Happy Family

WENDY LEE

Black Cat
New York

a paperback original imprint of Grove/Atlantic, Inc.

Published simultaneously in Canada
Printed in the United States of America

FIRST EDITION

ISBN-10: 0-8021-7046-3
ISBN-13: 978-0-8021-7046-0

Black Cat
a paperback original imprint of Grove/Atlantic, Inc.
841 Broadway
New York, NY 10003

Distributed by Publishers Group West

www.groveatlantic.com

08 09 10 11 12   10 9 8 7 6 5 4 3 2 1

*For my parents and in
the memory of my grandfather*

Prologue

Dear Lily,

I am writing to you from the beach in California. It is the middle of winter, but it is warm where I am. The sun glinting off the water shines in my eyes and makes the whole world look bright. Children run past, laughing. I watch as their legs scissor through the sand and into the water. The words are on the tip of my tongue—Be careful! Watch out! Don't run too fast! Then I remember that it is no longer my job to take care of children.

The sun warms the top of my head and spreads through my body. It is hard for me to remember how cold I was in New York, when I first met you. I wonder if you would recognize me now. My skin has grown tan, and squint lines have appeared around my eyes. My accent has faded, and the books that I take with me to read on the beach are all in English.

I wonder if I would recognize you. You will be four, maybe preparing to lose your first tooth. Do you remember the few months when

I cared for you, put you to bed in a room filled with toys, played with you in the park that was bordered by brownstones?

I have thought many times of writing to you about my new life, Lily. During the day, I clean houses. Sometimes, when my back aches, I think about my old job as a waitress. Except now I don't see the people I am working for, just the objects in their lives. I see their clothes and photographs, the books they think they should be reading, the things that turn these structures of glass and wood into their homes.

At one time in my life, I would have been tempted to take something small just to see if it would be noticed. But I can't risk losing my job, so I pick things up and put them down with impersonal hands. While I do, I think about how I don't have anything of yours, not a baby shoe or a lock of hair, or even a picture. I would like to at least have a picture.

At night I go to a business class for immigrants at a community college. Among the students are an Indian man who wants to buy a hardware store and a woman from El Salvador who wants to start her own bakery. Some of them are uneducated; some have been to college in their home countries and now have to start over. But we don't talk about our pasts, only the things we plan to do in the future. Everyone wants to come up with a good business proposal, so that if they can't get rich in their lifetimes, their children will.

After class I take the bus back to the home of my good friend Ah Jing. You didn't know her. We worked together, but she left for California before I met you and your mother. I have been sleeping on the couch in their living room for these past months. But she and her husband are expecting a baby, so I have to leave soon. They will insist that I stay, but they need the space to raise their own family. I've come to learn the importance of that, the room that is necessary for a family to grow and live and breathe. Sometimes I can hear them talking through the thin wall of their bedroom. Ah Jing wants a boy, but her husband hopes for a girl. Either way, the baby will be loved.

You were loved, too. You were loved by strangers from the moment they saw you, first your parents and then me. I hope that by now your parents have forgiven me for loving you as much as they did. If they are still married, maybe they would even thank me.

The sun is going down now and the sand is getting cold. The water has turned a different color, more gray than blue. But there is enough light for me to see where the sea meets the sky. Sometimes I think that if I were blessed with special vision, I would be able to see across the Pacific Ocean to China. And if I turned in the other direction, I would be able to see across the country, to you in New York, even across the past two years to the day I first met you.

With love,
Hua

Part I

Chapter One

I first met Lily and her mother in late winter, about three months after I had arrived in America. In that time, I had established a routine. Every day I took the same path from the boardinghouse where I lived to the restaurant where I worked, and back again. Once a week, on my half day off, I walked toward the water so that the breeze would carry away the oily smell in my hair and the customers' voices ringing in my ears. I went south to Battery Park, where I watched the ferries loaded with tourists heading for Ellis Island. Or I walked east underneath the Manhattan Bridge, with the traffic rushing overhead, or west to the Hudson River opposite the New Jersey shoreline where boats passed with their white sails aloft.

On my trip over to America, I'd comforted myself with the thought that I would be going to live in a place near the water. I was from Fuzhou, a city on the southeastern coast of China that was bisected by a river that ran to the ocean. I'd lived in the part of the city that lay on an island so large you couldn't tell you were on an island, except that the main sprawl of the city shone across the water. So I told myself that Manhattan was only an island, too, no matter how large or inhospitable.

But that winter day, I decided to walk north toward the interior of the city. The frigid weather did little to temper the smells of the Chinatown streets, of garbage and food scraps and rotting fruit. Piles of snow that had fallen weeks before had turned dark and rank, like the ice packed around fish in the markets. Crisp air outlined the buildings and sharpened the honking of car horns and the sound of trucks rumbling down from the bridge. I dug my hands into the pockets of my worn black coat and crossed Canal Street into Little Italy.

Across Broadway, tenements gave way to the cast-iron fronts of buildings with stores below and apartments above. These stores were devoted to single, specific things: clothes for children, coats for dogs, bathroom soaps, French tarts. As I headed west, there were fewer stores and more houses, brownstones that rose four or five stories above the narrow, cobblestoned streets. Some buildings were covered with dead vines and had empty flower boxes in the windows. I tried to imagine what the street would look like in the spring when everything was green and growing. I decided it would look beautiful.

I rounded a corner and came upon a small park shaded by the bare branches of trees. In the other parks I had seen in this city, there were people in suits taking refuge from work, or students with books in their laps, or homeless men sleeping in the sun. In this park, there were only women and children. As I got closer, I saw that these women were not all mothers, or at least not the mothers of the children they were looking after. Their dark eyes rested upon children with skin lighter than their own. Some sat in silence on the benches, while others chatted with each other in sharp-angled languages.

I sat down on a bench and joined in watching the activity before me on the playground. The children appeared fearless. They flung themselves off the swings and down the slides as if confident that someone would be there to catch them. A blond-haired boy chased a girl around the perimeter of the playground until I was sure he would make her trip. In the next moment, they had switched places and she was chasing him. On the other side of the playground, a little boy did trip. He opened his mouth to howl, looking toward the bench where his nanny was sitting. But the woman, whose skin was like wrinkled brown silk, continued to chat with her friend and knit. Her needles flashed through the fine wool of a sweater that looked like it was being made for a larger child, perhaps her own. The little boy closed his mouth and got up without a sound.

The children who were playing alone fascinated me the most. I watched a little girl with glasses gathering twigs, a boy building a tower out of smooth stones. Another girl appeared to be having a conversation with someone only she could see, an imaginary friend more interesting than any of her real-life playmates. I had always played alone as a child. I didn't have any brothers or sisters, or children my age living nearby. My grandmother never bothered to supervise me. The trouble I'd get into, she said, I'd get into anyway. Like most children, I played in the narrow winding streets or along the banks of the river.

I closed my eyes, thinking of the small park that I could see from my grandmother's house. Every morning, our next-door neighbor would go outside with a songbird in a bamboo cage. He would hang the cage on a tree branch and begin his morning exercises. His arms would trace circles in the hazy dawn as dust rose in clouds around his feet. Other elderly people would

11

join him with their birds, and soon the park would be ringed with cages. As a child I imagined that the birds sang from the joy of being outside. Then, when I was older, I thought it was cruel to give the birds just a glimpse of the world from the imprisonment of their cages. Or maybe that one glimpse was enough. I had never been able to decide.

I opened my eyes to see a woman pushing a little girl in a stroller toward my bench. In their own way, they looked as mismatched as any of the other women and children. The woman was American, tall, with red hair shining above an expensive-looking cream-colored coat. The little girl was Chinese, with black hair cut straight across her forehead, and eyebrows so thick they resembled caterpillars. She wore a pink coat and appeared to be around two years old. When they reached the other end of the bench, the woman gave me a small smile. The little girl looked at me with her thick, dark brows drawn together as if in disapproval. There was something familiar about that look, and I wondered if I'd had the same one on my face when I was a child. Maybe, in some way, the girl recognized that she looked like me.

"Do you want to go play?" the woman asked.

An emphatic nod.

"Go ahead, then. I'll watch from here."

The little girl walked toward the other children, taking one uncertain step after the other. The woman opened a book in her lap, but her eyes never left the little girl, as if somehow the sight of the child kept her warm and breathing. That was how I knew, more than anything else, that no matter how different they looked from each other, these two were mother and daughter.

After a moment, the little girl turned around and came back toward her mother. As she got closer, the woman pretended to be absorbed in her book, although a smile remained in the corner of her mouth. It seemed to be a game between them; the little girl tried to get her mother's attention while her mother pretended not to see her. Finally she grabbed the woman's hand and tugged on it.

"Shall we go on the swings?" A smile spread across the little girl's face as if nothing could make her happier. The woman glanced at her watch. "All right, just for a few minutes."

She placed the book facedown and took the little girl's hand, leaving her bag on the bench. I looked around to see if anyone else had noticed. Surely she didn't mean to leave her bag where someone could take it. Or maybe she trusted me to look after it. At that thought my hands twitched despite themselves. I wanted to turn the book right side up to see what she was reading, to go through her bag and see what else was inside. I went so far as to turn my head so that I could see what was on the cover of the book. To my surprise, it was a history of Chinese brush painting during the Tang Dynasty.

The woman was pushing the little girl higher on the swing. The arc of her arm and the girl's flying body made a complete motion, as if a current was passing between them. With her short, paintbrush braids, the little girl reminded me of the child I had often seen on government billboards back home, advertising the desirability of having a girl over a boy, to combat traditional views. This image featured a young couple, the father in a suit and the mother in a blouse and skirt. They held the hands of a little girl wearing a school uniform, her pigtails dancing. Everyone was smiling, their cheeks spots of red. The only thing I had in common with the little girl on the billboard was that I was also an only child. At that age my hair had never been allowed to grow past my chin, and my cheeks never got that red unless it was the middle of winter. And, of course, by the time I was old enough to go to school, my parents were dead. They were killed in a factory fire when I was three years old, and my grandmother had brought me up.

Now I noticed that different children were on the swings. I looked around to see that the woman and the little girl were returning to the bench. I moved closer to my end so the woman wouldn't think I had been looking through her things. She moved past me without a glance and started packing up her bag. Once the little girl had been settled in her stroller, the two moved back the way they had come.

Then I spotted something lying underneath the bench. It was tiny and pink, like a flower or a person's ear. I picked it up and brushed it off, and discovered that it was a child's mitten. I remembered its mate on the little girl's hand; it was the exact shade of pink as her coat. For a second I thought about putting the mitten in my pocket. The little girl's mother wouldn't notice it was missing until they got home, and the girl probably had a drawerful of mittens to choose from. I wanted something to remember the little girl and her mother by, in case I never saw them again. Then it occurred to me that they would never remember me unless I did something to make them remember.

"Excuse me," I called. The little girl and her mother didn't turn around. I bit my lip and ran after them. "Excuse me!"

I held the mitten out in response to the woman's questioning look, my tongue suddenly clumsy. "This—is yours?"

"Yes," the woman said, the creases around her eyes deepening as she took the mitten. At this proximity I could see that she was older than I had originally thought, perhaps in her early forties. "Thank you." She turned to the little girl. "Say thank you, Lily."

The girl stared at me from beneath those ridiculously thick brows.

"Say thank you to the nice lady," her mother prompted.

"Thank you," Lily whispered, and then hid her face as if too shy to look at me again.

I watched them until the cream-colored blur of the woman's coat disappeared at the end of the street. Shivering a little, I realized it was time for me to go, too. It was getting late. The sun had dipped behind the brownstones, and the shadows of the children on the swings were lengthening with each flash across the asphalt. I had the walk to Chinatown ahead of me.

A few blocks away from the park, I looked up to see what the names of the streets were so that I could return if I wanted to. I recited them over and over in my head: Greenwich and Jane.

Chapter Two

As I walked home, the quiet rows of brownstones soon gave way to noisy commercial streets and then, finally, the bustle that was Chinatown. Even though it was a weekday, tourists crowded the sidewalks of Canal Street, dazzled by pirated CDs, fake designer purses, and discounted perfumes. Mothers hurried children home from school. Elderly women were out in force to finish their shopping for the day, moving at a shuffle in quiet defiance of normal traffic. Sometimes I imagined my grandmother was among these women. A tiny figure with the same determined angle to her chin, the gleam in her eyes that missed nothing. She'd be carrying a bag of clementines to bring to a sick friend, or fresh crab and sticky rice to make my favorite dish.

"Hua," she would say to me, "are you back from school already?"

"No, Po Po," I would reply, "I just came to meet you, to help you carry your bags home."

Then I would shake my head to remind myself that my grandmother was back in China, and that these other women on the street were someone else's grandmother.

I paused at a produce stand to look at the vegetables, the green hairy-skinned melons and eggplant as slender as my arm, the long beans that trailed like locks of hair. My grandmother would cook the beans with slices of salty pork, and they would be tastier than at any restaurant in Chinatown. She had a hand with cooking that made every dish here taste like sand.

All around me on Canal Street people spoke in Cantonese, the language of the south of China. It always sounded to me like someone speaking through a mouthful of dried peas.

Fujianese, the dialect that was more familiar to my tongue, was spoken on East Broadway in Chinatown, but everyone at the restaurant where I worked spoke Cantonese except for the owner. He was from Beijing and, like me, spoke Mandarin. When the other workers grumbled behind his back, I could never understand what they were saying. Ah Jing, one of the waitresses who had become my friend, explained to me what they were talking about: his gambling, the money he owed, family problems. But a month ago Ah Jing and her husband had moved to California, so now there was no one at the restaurant I could talk to. Although I had picked up some Cantonese phrases, I knew more English, which I had studied in school, than the language spoken by most of the people around me. Sometimes when I walked down the street, listening to the strange mix of languages and dialects, I felt like I was living in an entirely different country, neither the China I knew nor the America I had envisioned.

I lingered in the streets until my fingers grew cold. I wasn't eager to get back to my boardinghouse room. The only thing to look forward to was to see if I had received any letters, and

they could only be from three people: Ah Jing; my old classmate Swallow; or my grandmother. The boardinghouse on
Bayard Street was owned by a Mrs. Ma. She lived in the apartment on the first floor, below my room, and often had people
over to play mah-jongg late into the night. I would wake up
to hear the waterfall of clicking sounds as the tiles were being
shuffled.

Now, as I entered the hallway, I could tell that something
important was going on in the Ma household. The door to
the apartment was open and I could hear voices speaking in
Cantonese issuing forth. Even though I couldn't understand
what was being said, there was a festive air to it. I lingered at
the edge of the noise, not sure if I should go in.

Mrs. Ma came to meet me, closing the door partway behind her so that just a slice of the light and voices came through.
It must have been a special occasion, because instead of her
usual polyester outfit and ratty cloth slippers she was wearing
an embroidered dress with matching shoes, their red a shade
too youthful for her graying hair.

"Oh, hello, Hua," Mrs. Ma said in Mandarin. "Was there
something you wanted?"

"I was wondering if any mail had come for me," I said.
Usually Mrs. Ma left her tenants' mail out on the table in the
hall, but I hadn't seen anything when I came in.

"Yes, I haven't had a chance to put it out today," she said.
"We've been quite busy here, as you can see. My daughter
just got engaged."

"Oh. *Gongxi ni,*" I added politely.

Mrs. Ma smiled at my congratulations. "Wait here." She
went back inside, leaving the door slightly open.

I remained where I was, leaning against the wall where
the light from the doorway cut across my face. I had seen

Mrs. Ma's daughter before, a plain-faced woman in her early thirties. It was probably a relief for both her and her mother that she was getting married. She was a good daughter who often brought bulging grocery bags and pink bakery boxes to her mother's house.

The door opened wider and Mrs. Ma handed me a single postcard that I knew could only be from Ah Jing.

"Thank you," I said, trying not to show how much I wanted to be alone so I could read it.

"Don't be so polite." Mrs. Ma paused. I could see a crowd of people behind her, talking and eating. I picked out the plain-faced daughter, and I thought her face was not so plain now as she turned to a man in a dark suit who must be her fiancé.

"Have you eaten yet?" Mrs. Ma asked.

"I've eaten already, thank you," I said in a rush.

"All right, then." Mrs. Ma gave me another long look and the door closed behind her. For a moment, in the darkness of the hall, I felt a twinge of regret. The room had seemed so alive with the talking, even if it was in a language I couldn't understand. But Mrs. Ma's look had indicated pity, and I couldn't bear anyone feeling sorry for me. I remembered the postcard in my hand and hurried upstairs.

There were six doors on my floor, three facing three across the narrow carpeted hall. Although I didn't know the other boarders very well by sight—I usually hurried in and out, closing my door quickly behind me—I knew the sounds they made. There was a man who plucked out unsteady notes on a guitar, another who shuffled down the hall as though he wore shoes made of lead. There was a woman who always listened to the radio in the morning, and another who sometimes, late at night, would let loose a cry from either pleasure or pain, I couldn't tell which.

Once inside my room, I turned on the light. The bulb lit a space that was furnished with as little as could be gotten away with: a twin bed, a small table, a chair. I figured the pieces had come from Mrs. Ma's daughter's room. It was really just a bedroom. There was no kitchen so I ate at the restaurant, and there was a shared bathroom at the end of the hall. Usually the smallness and shabbiness of the room pressed down on me once I entered it, but I didn't notice that day.

I flung myself stomach down on the bed and turned the postcard to the front. The giant, human-like figures of a mouse and a duck were standing in front of a castle, waving. I traced the words across the top with my finger: Greetings from Disneyland!

Dear Hua, Ah Jing wrote in small, spidery Chinese characters to economize the space. *My sister-in-law and her husband are crazy. They spend all their time working and Pei and I have to take care of the kids. And the kids are completely spoiled, don't speak any Chinese, and refuse to eat anything I cook. But my sister-in-law has finally found us work in a factory, sewing clothes. We start in a week. I hear it is harder than working in a restaurant, but at least you get the chance to sit down, right? I hope business is well at the restaurant. Don't let anyone there push you around. It really does feel like summer here.*

I read the postcard again, then a third time, savoring Ah Jing's bad handwriting. Then I tacked it on the wall above my bed, beside the other three postcards I had received from her in the month she'd been gone. They were all from California and featured some combination of palm trees, a bright sun, and a beach.

Before she moved, Ah Jing and I had talked about what her new life in California would be like. Late at night at the restaurant, when there were no customers but before our boss allowed us to close, we'd sneak out into the alleyway where only a square of starless sky was visible because of the surrounding buildings. We were cold without our coats, but we'd stay out there anyway, shivering and talking about warmer climates.

"It's summer year-round in California," I'd start. "The magazines say so."

"It'd better be." Ah Jing's breath was a puff in the dark. She was from Guangdong Province, farther south than where I was from, and was even less able to deal with the cold. "What else do your magazines say?"

I closed my eyes and waved my hands as if I were a fortune-teller. "You'll live in a large house with a pool and a garden. You'll have ten bedrooms and a room just for the maid."

"No way," Ah Jing said. "We're not movie stars. We're going to be living with Pei's sister and husband and their kids."

My eyes flew open. "Well, it must be big if both you and Pei can stay there."

"That's true."

"You'll get burned black from spending too much time in the sun."

"I'll drive my own car on the freeway."

We were both so cold by then that we were jumping up and down to keep warm.

"I'll pick oranges from trees in my backyard!" Ah Jing kicked an old crate as punctuation to her sentence.

"You'll go swimming in the ocean every day!" I kicked another crate and the wood splintered with a crash.

"Hey!" someone called from a window above. "Too noisy down there!"

Ah Jing and I covered our mouths to keep from giggling and ran back in to the restaurant, where we immediately wrapped our hands around stainless-steel teapots to thaw them out.

~   ~   ~

Whenever Ah Jing and I had talked about California, speculating and dreaming as if it were another country, I felt like I was with Swallow, my best friend and classmate from Fuzhou. Swallow and I would often wonder what it would be like to live in America, how big one's house would be, whether one would drive a car, if one would have to own a gun to stay safe. Swallow was convinced one would have to have a gun, but then she was always the most cautious of all my classmates.

We would discuss this in our college dormitory after the lights went out at ten-thirty, when most of the other girls were whispering and gossiping about our handsome new literature teacher. That dorm room was no larger than the room I now rented at Mrs. Ma's, but it had four bunk beds against the walls and a table with chairs in the middle for studying. Some girls would drape mosquito netting around their beds, as much for privacy as to ward off the bugs, but there was no escaping the constant presence of other people. I didn't mind it, though. I even missed the way the air in the room would feel heavy in the middle of the night from everyone's breathing.

We all thought Swallow's name suited her because she was small and round, her short hair as glossy as a bird's wing. Our teachers smiled upon her even though she wasn't very good at her lessons. Up until our third and last year in school, I had to help her in most of her classes, especially English, which was my best subject. Swallow's father was some kind of government official—exactly what he did, even Swallow didn't know. But on Saturdays she was picked up by a driver and taken to an apartment complex of white and pink tile, still so new that there were traces of putty on the windowpanes. Sometimes I went there with her to spend the weekend, and we would watch variety shows on her family's large color television or go downtown. At night I slept next to her in her double bed, close enough for our dreams to intermingle.

Before I left for America, we met one last time at her house. I had heard that she was working as a tea girl at her father's office. This meant that whenever there were meetings between the heads of different prefectures, Swallow would bring in lidded porcelain cups of tea and stand in the background with a thermos of hot water to keep them filled. She was also responsible for arranging the white cloths draped over the backs of the armchairs and emptying the ashtrays and spittoons. It was not much better than a secretary's job, despite her father's influence.

Swallow showed me the uniform she got to wear: a starched white shirt, a red skirt, and a sash to be worn over the chest. She draped the sash over my head and I pretended to march like a soldier. Then I did the same to her, and she beamed and waved like a beauty-pageant contestant. We both burst into laughter.

"I'm sorry you're going away," Swallow said, abruptly serious.

"Maybe you can go, too, someday. Your father will arrange it."

"You don't have to leave China anymore to be successful. People who go to school in the States come back and start businesses and get rich." Swallow sounded like an echo of her father, who often talked about the potential of the New China. "Besides," she added, "I wouldn't want to go right now."

"Why not?"

At this, Swallow blushed, and I knew why it didn't matter that she had a meaningless job that required her to just stand around and look pretty. She had a boyfriend.

"What's his name?"

"Zhongmin."

Faithful to the People. It was a very patriotic name. I could imagine him in short pants as a child, the class monitor's red bandanna around his neck, running around the school playground and threatening to tell the teacher on his classmates.

"My parents like him," Swallow rushed on. "He works in the accounting department, and he'll probably be promoted by next year. His family owns several shoe stores in town."

"He sounds very nice." I didn't know what else to say.

"He is."

I could see Swallow's life: living with her parents in that pink-and-white tiled apartment complex until she got married, then moving to a similar building with her patriotically named husband, having a child, keeping the same government job until she retired, and then taking care of her grandchild until she was no longer useful. In some ways it would be such an easy life. For one thing, she would never have to be alone.

As I looked at the tea-girl uniform spread across Swallow's bed, I was flooded with jealousy. Life had always been so simple for her. When I had been invited to her house, I could feel some advantage over her because I had been better at my studies. But now that period in our lives was finished, and it was obvious what she had and what I didn't. She had a job, a boyfriend, a family, a future here. I had only the promise of a future in America.

Swallow misinterpreted the look on my face and touched my shoulder, concerned. "Are you afraid to leave home?" she asked.

I thought of my grandmother and the small house I had grown up in, the damp gray winters and the sweltering summers, the rows of laundry that never quite dried. The old man at the bottom of the hill who fixed shoes, the vendors who sold bananas inside tunnels that had been used as bomb shelters during wartime. The statue of Mao in the town square with his arm uplifted, welcoming you home.

"I don't know," I said.

The end of our visit came, and Swallow and I promised we would write each other.

She had written often in the beginning, but then the letters had trailed off. They hadn't been that interesting anyway, mostly about her new boyfriend and the dull places they went to on dates, like the local McDonald's and West Lake Park. I also didn't have much to write about. I didn't want her to know how different my life here was from the way we'd imagined it.

~   ~   ~

I kept Swallow's letters in a suitcase under my bed along with the letters from my grandmother, which always began the same way. My grandmother would thank me for the money I had sent the month before and then write about the ordinary things that had happened to her that day: if the fish had been fresh, if she'd had a particularly difficult customer who wanted something mended at once. My grandmother was a seamstress, although she did less work now that her hands were seizing up with arthritis and the eyestrain gave her headaches. I could imagine her sitting at the kitchen table, writing carefully and slowly in her long, capable hand. When I thought about this, homesickness would well up in my throat.

I had felt homesick only once before in my life, and it wasn't for my parents.

At the time of the fire that claimed my parents' lives, I was already being raised by my grandmother in Fuzhou. Both my parents worked in a government-run factory located several miles out of town. They lived in separate dormitories on the factory grounds and would take the bus home on weekends. I remembered them only as pleasant blurs: a man who would hold me up under the low ceiling of the living room, a woman whose laughter rang in my ears like running water. It was my grandmother's hands that tucked the blanket under my chin before I went to sleep, her voice that soothed me after I woke from a bad dream.

My grandmother's house was modest, just two rooms with whitewashed walls, on a narrow winding road at the end of a row of shops. It was warmed in the winter by a foul-smelling, coal-burning stove and cooled in the summer by an electric fan. The furniture was mostly plain and utilitarian, stuff that you could find in any of our neighbor's households, but there were also a few pieces made out of rosewood, at odds with the rest of the room. No one but company was allowed to use this furniture; most of the time it sat there as if in a museum. I was allowed to touch it only when I dusted, and I couldn't just run a damp rag along the table legs. I had to wipe each delicately carved curlicue until it shone deep red, like congealed blood.

When I was a child, my grandmother walked me to the primary school every day to make sure I got there on time. I lagged because I didn't want to be in school, where I was ahead of my classmates. I spent most of the day staring out the window at the hills beyond, sometimes following a single farmer and his ox until they disappeared into a valley. In the morning

I did whatever I could to be late, from tearing a hole in my clothes to claiming that I had lost my pencil. My grandmother would end up having to hustle us along so I wouldn't be late.

In the afternoon, though, I was allowed to come home on my own, and I would take the long way. I'd wander alone down roads lined with banyan trees, the roots drifting from the branches like the beards of old men. There was one huge tree in particular that was rumored to be haunted. I always ran past it, screaming, in case a bony hand would emerge from the dark hollow in the trunk and grab me.

The best part of the walk was when I passed by the house that looked different from any other in town. This house was large and built in the Western style with wide, shuttered windows and a tiled roof whose eaves pointed straight down instead of swooping toward the sky. It was set back from the road and surrounded by stone walls studded at the top with broken glass. Visible over the walls were plum trees, spiky branches in the winter and bloom-white in the spring. But aside from the trees there was no sign of life. The windows were boarded up and weeds grew between the crevices in the wall. It didn't look like anyone had lived there for years. I often wondered who owned the place, and my mind filled with the Western fairy tales I knew about imprisoned princesses and rich merchants who had lost their fortunes.

One day I was sitting at the kitchen table watching my grandmother chop cabbage for dinner. Her left hand curled the cabbage head toward her so that the side of the knife hit her knuckles first; that way she wouldn't cut herself.

"Po Po," I said, "what is that house with the funny roof?"

The knife paused mid-slice, the crinkled, pale green leaves falling like confetti. "We once lived in that house," my grandmother said. "It belonged to your grandfather and me. He was

so proud of being able to build a house like those in the foreign concession in Shanghai. The glass in the windows was
imported from Hong Kong."

"What happened? Why did you leave?"

"We didn't leave," she corrected me. "We were forced out
by a local cadre and his family. At first we were told we could
stay if we worked for them. So I was a cook and your grandfather was a handyman."

"Is that how Ye Ye got sick?" I asked.

"Yes, his lungs were always weak and he couldn't take our
new way of living. I also think he couldn't bear the idea of
other people living in his house."

"Do you still own the house?"

"Of course not. When the cadre and his family moved to
Shanghai, after your grandfather died, the property was turned
over to the state. Before the house was boarded up, our old
neighbors helped us sneak out the furniture piece by piece."

I was silent for a moment as I watched my grandmother
resume chopping cabbage. My heart felt as heavy as each stroke
of the knife. "Why didn't you tell me this before?"

My grandmother shrugged, a gentle rise and fall of her shoulders. "What use would that be? What's lost is lost."

Later I would understand what my grandmother meant, why
it would be useless to think about what could have happened
if our house hadn't been taken away. For anything different
to have happened, the entire course of history would have had
to be changed. Our lives weren't the only ones affected, and
many people had lost more—members of their family, an entire
lineage wiped out. But still, I felt homesick for that Western-
style house on the hill, a place I had never seen the inside of.

Later I would learn of other things that had been lost during the Cultural Revolution, like my grandmother's hopes for

my mother. My grandmother, who came from a good family involved in overseas trading, had learned English and French as a student in Shanghai. This was before the Japanese Occupation, when students were encouraged to study abroad. She had wanted to go overseas but then the civil war came, and for the next thirty years the country was clamped shut, she liked to say, like a locked box without a key.

While my grandparents were virtually under house arrest, my mother was sent into the mountains of southwest China for reeducation. She was only a secondary-school student and had never been away from home before. At the camps she met my father, who was from Manchuria, in the northern part of the country. After their reeducation was complete, they came back to my mother's hometown, where my grandmother was living, like everyone else, in a tiny house with whitewashed walls, and got married.

While my mother was growing up, my grandmother kept a trunk filled with satin *qipaos* for my mother to wear on her wedding day, embroidered quilts with matching pillowcases, and brocade tablecloths that were supposed to be part of her dowry. But in my parents' wedding picture, there's no sign of that luxury. My mother and father are standing next to each other, straight and correct, not even touching. They're both wearing almost identical uniforms, with matching caps and bandannas around their neck; my mother's hair is tied back. They look unaware of the importance of what has just occurred.

Whenever I looked at that picture, I could feel the weight of everything that came before and after. If it weren't for my grandparents losing their house and my mother being sent away, my parents would never have met, and I would never have been born. And if my parents hadn't spent their youth in the reeducation camps, they wouldn't have been forced to take jobs in a textile factory, the only work left for people like them. They wouldn't have been there the day the fire broke out.

There was more that was expected of me. Since as long as I could remember, my grandmother had wanted me to go to America. I had started learning English at the age of twelve, at school. My college entrance exam scores were not high enough to get me into the top-tier schools in Beijing or Shanghai, but good enough for the three-year private girls' college in town, below the hill where we lived, where I continued to learn English. The college had been started in the mid-nineteenth century by American missionaries, and remnants of that history were everywhere—in the ornate ceiling of the auditorium that had once been a chapel, in the hymns that some of the teachers taught—even if nothing was allowed to be overtly religious.

Certainly, when I was doing so poorly in my last year at school, I would pray to any god to let me pass my final exams and graduate. But there was no hope for me. My failure was such that I could hardly look my grandmother in the face. All the money she had saved to put me through school was wasted. She had hoped I might win one of the few scholarships that allowed college graduates to go overseas each year, but without a degree or family connections I didn't have a chance. There was only one other way to get to America, which had already proved so popular that some villages along the coast had nearly no men of working age left. Almost everyone had a relative or knew someone who had emigrated illegally. It was, people said, in our blood to leave for distant shores.

My grandmother told me I had an aunt and uncle on my father's side who lived in New Jersey. Their family had gone to Taiwan after the Communists had come into power and then, later, to the States. They had helped numerous other family members leave the country, partly out of guilt for having escaped all the bad things that had happened under the Communists. My grandmother wrote them and they agreed to be the sponsors for my illegal passage.

Next she found people in Fuzhou who would arrange for my trip to America. For what exact price I didn't know, although I knew that transportation fees weren't cheap. People spent years paying off their debts to the so-called snakeheads, or else their families back home did. My grandmother refused to tell me, saying that she had some money saved up, and my uncle and aunt in New Jersey were helping out, and that she even had a little left over from the government compensation for my parents' death.

The day before I was to leave on a bus that would take me to Shenzhen, the booming town on the border between China and Hong Kong, my grandmother and I made a pilgrimage to the cemetery where my parents and grandfather were buried. It was atop a hill on the outskirts of town, where on a good day you could see the ocean. That day, though, the sky was dark with impending rain, and the seagulls had come in from the coast. We came to this place every spring for the tomb-sweeping holiday, the day on which you were supposed to tend your ancestors' graves. But who knew when I would come here next. I had to make up for what could be years of absence in one afternoon.

I watched as my grandmother went through the prayer ritual, bowing deeply before each grave. Then it was my turn. I took the three lighted incense sticks she handed me and knelt in front of my grandfather's grave. I had never met him, didn't even know how to think of him outside of this place, even though I called him Ye Ye. I quickly bowed three times and then took the next trio of incense sticks from my grandmother. These were for my parents; they'd share them, as they had so many things throughout their lives, including their moment of death.

My grandmother came up behind me as I stood and brushed the dirt from my knees. "Too bad you've never been up north to visit your other grandparents' grave," she said matter-of-factly. "It's bad luck to leave the country without paying respects to both sides of the family."

"Where are they buried?" I asked.

"In Ha'erbin," she said. "They were good people. They offered to take you in after your parents died, but I thought it would be easier for you to stay here. They have different ways of doing things up north. They eat bread instead of rice, and you ate a lot of rice as a child."

I smiled, used to my grandmother's odd rationalizations. I knew what she meant. "But at least they wanted me," I teased.

My grandmother looked cross. "Who says no one wanted you? You were very much wanted, by both sides of the family. Not all children who lose their parents are that lucky."

"I wouldn't have wanted to go to Ha'erbin anyway," I said. "It's too cold there."

"That's true. But your father's family are Wus, they can stand any kind of hardship." My grandmother looked at me keenly. "You're a Wu, too, remember that."

"What about your family?" I asked. "Aren't they strong?"

"It's a different kind of strength. The Chengs are known for bending in the breeze, for giving in to others. That's how they get what they want. And that's what you have to do when you get to America. You have to be what other people want you to be, before you can be yourself. Then you'll do both of our families proud."

I nodded, swallowing hard. I thought about the false promises of my grandmother's youth, her arranged marriage, her missed chance to study overseas, the dowry she would never get to pass on to her daughter. This was also true of my mother, who had been hundreds of miles away when her own father died, and who had not been able to see me grow up. I had added to this legacy by failing to graduate, and with all the trouble in the past year that had strained the relationship between my grandmother and me. If I stayed, I would be nothing but shame to my family. I had to make all of this right.

"Besides," my grandmother added, "there's nothing left for you here."

"There's you," I said.

"I won't be here forever. When I'm gone, what will you do? What can I leave you that's worth more than this?"

I turned away and looked at the surrounding tombstones crumbling back into the earth, the green hillside, the darkness of the sky and the sea beyond.

"Someday," my grandmother said, "you'll come back with your children and you'll take care of these family graves. I'll be snug beside your grandfather by then. But promise me you won't forget to do this."

My grandmother knelt at the foot of my grandfather's grave and took a flask out of the bag she carried. After pouring the clear liquid into a tiny porcelain cup, she toasted the headstone, then poured it onto the ground. The grain liquor seeped into the soil, where it would reach the dead.

"Your grandfather always did like his *baijiu*," she said.

"I promise," I said.

~ ~ ~

It was late at night now. I lay in bed underneath a thin coverlet, thinking about the different places I could remember having slept: in my grandmother's house, the apartment of Swallow's family, the dorm room at school. I missed the heavy cotton layers of those blankets. I heard the building settle around me, the soft thuds of doors banging shut, floorboards creaking beneath feet, the unmistakable clicking of mah-jongg tiles being shuffled from the apartment below. Though most of Mrs. Ma's guests had probably left hours ago, no party was complete without a little gambling. The sounds reminded me irrevocably of where I was, in Chinatown, in New York, in America. Even in the darkness with my eyes closed, I couldn't imagine myself out of this place.

Then my mind expanded as I thought of the little girl I had seen in the park that afternoon. I followed her down the street to the front of a building, up the brownstone facade, and through a window into her bedroom. There she lay, fast asleep, not knowing she was so far away from home.

Chapter Three

When spring finally came, the markets in Chinatown began selling loquats that were small and hard, like babies' curled fists. The windows of the building facing mine at the boardinghouse were left open at night, and I could hear voices and radio music rising in the night air after I went to bed. As I stood at the back door of the restaurant where I worked, I could smell the trash bags that lined the alley, the odor of garbage loosened by the afternoon sun.

In the park near Greenwich and Jane, spring was evident in the pale green buds on the trees and the daffodils that bloomed at their bases, and in the children who ran across the playground unburdened by winter clothes. Since seeing Lily and her mother, I had gone back to the park every week on my half day off, but they hadn't shown up again. Still, I went and waited at the bench where I had first seen them. Even the anticipation that I might see them carried me through the days of work and dark nights.

One afternoon, just as I was leaving the restaurant at the end of my shift, I heard a shout from the kitchen. I turned and saw the long, thin body of one of the cooks, a man named Li, bent double over the metal counter. The towel wrapped around his hand looked as though it were draining all of the color from his normally ruddy face.

Old Chou, our boss, was right behind me, his mouth already opening to shout at us to get back to work. Then he saw the red stain that spread down Li's arm.

"What happened?"

Li motioned with his chin toward the counter where a knife lay next to a pile of red-roasted pork. "I think it's in there."

"What?"

"The rest of my finger!"

Gao, the second cook, laughed. "Just throw everything in." He shook the pan of green peppers on the stove in front of him. "No one will notice."

Old Chou poked around the meat slices with his own finger. "I see it. Just a piece of skin. Not worth saving."

We all leaned in closer. I could see something that looked like the tiny half of a shriveled peanut. It was already hard to imagine as being the tip of someone's finger. I felt someone breathing down my neck and turned to see the Mexican dishwasher, Miguel, who couldn't possibly have understood what anyone was saying.

"I seen worse," Miguel said and went back to the sink.

"Shouldn't he go to the hospital?" I said.

"No hospital!" Old Chou glared at me as if I had suggested going to the police. He grabbed Li's wrist and turned the injured hand up. "Look! The bleeding is slowing down."

I watched Li for his reaction, but he merely shrugged. He looked stronger now, the color returning to his face.

"Too bad about your finger, Li," Gao smirked. "Maybe you won't become a famous musician after all, eh?"

Li scowled at this. He played classical Spanish guitar, which he had learned from listening to old records back home in Hong Kong. Sometimes he stayed up late to practice and came to work half asleep, and then he wielded the cleaver as if in a dream.

"Enough of that," Old Chou said. "You go home for the rest of the day," he told Li. "Gao, stop sounding like an idiot and get back to work. And you—"

"It's the end of my shift," I informed him before he could think of something useful for me to do. But as I turned, I ran into the other waitress, Xiao Ru, who was coming into the kitchen with a stack of dirty dishes. I put out my own hands to steady her and the edges of the plates hit the insides of my elbows. Xiao Ru took one look over my shoulder at the blood-ied towel around Li's arm and had to sit down, her face paler than the injured cook's.

Instantly the lines in Old Chou's face softened. Xiao Ru seemed to have that effect on everyone at the restaurant except me. To me she was just the person who had replaced my friend Ah Jing, but Li and Gao competed with each other to clean up after her spills and hide her broken dishes, and even Miguel had once given her a half-dead flower he'd found on the sidewalk. She was young and pretty, but Old Chou was gentle with her for a different reason. He couldn't have another waitress leave him so soon, not after she'd just about learned how to do every-thing properly. The first time he had yelled at her for spilling sauce on a white tablecloth, she'd burst into tears and was useless for the rest of the day. Now she just sniffled when reprimanded.

"You sit and rest," Old Chou told her. "You"—he turned his bristle-browed gaze to me—"take over for her until she feels well enough to work again."

I was about to protest but closed my mouth. I didn't want to get on Old Chou's bad side in case he decided to take away my half days off altogether. I looked at Xiao Ru, whose face was starting to look less white, and regretted that I had helped her. Then I remembered that I had been in her position when I had started working here and Ah Jing had shown me around.

"Thank you, elder sister," Xiao Ru whispered to me.

I bit back my immediate response, which had been to say that I wasn't much older than her. I knew she was only trying to be polite.

So Li went home with a heavily bandaged hand, Old Chou put on Li's apron, and Xiao Ru watched everything from a chair in the kitchen. I was sent out to the dining room with a dish of green peppers and red-roasted pork from which, hopefully, all the blood had been washed off. I deposited it on a table in front of a middle-aged American couple who looked too soured by life to possibly have anything left to say to each other. The man looked out of the window while the woman regarded me with the corners of her mouth tucked in, as if she had already tasted something bad.

"Can we get some more tea?" she said, tapping the empty pot. Her nail against the stainless steel made me cringe.

"Of course," I said.

"Well, I asked you once before when you took our order."

I stifled the urge to point out that a different waitress had been serving her then. I just took the teapot, ducking my head so that she couldn't see my face.

When I had first started working here, Ah Jing had told me, "If there is a customer you can't stand, you should spit in their tea. Or you can spit in their soup. Hot-and-sour works best."

"Really?" I'd said.

"They can't taste the difference. You could serve an old shoe as long as it was covered with oyster sauce and they wouldn't know. But you know who's worse than these *laowai*?"

I was surprised that Ah Jing referred to Americans as foreigners when we were the ones who were the true foreigners in this country. "Who?" I asked.

Ah Jing curled her lip. "*Meiji huaren.*"

Chinese-Americans. I had noticed how they either spoke slowly to make sure I could understand them and left meager tips or seemed embarrassed by my presence, as if I reminded them of a parent or relative who had started out the same way, and left big tips from guilt.

Finally, the sour-faced couple I had been serving finished their meal, down to the last fortune-cookie crumb and orange slice. They were the last from the noon crowd to leave, and I thankfully closed the door behind them and locked it. There were a few hours before we would open again for dinner, and Old Chou usually kept us busy wiping down tables or mopping the floors. Today, though, he looked as tired as everyone else. He announced that he would have us fold napkins, one of the easier tasks. Instantly Xiao Ru chirped that she was feeling better, and to my surprise, since we were still short-handed, Old Chou told me to take the rest of the day off.

For the second time that day I removed my apron and hung it on the rack of hooks next to the storage closet, across from the metal counters. Before I left I glanced through the swinging door that separated the kitchen and the dining room. This restaurant looked the same as any other on the block with its fish tanks of grimy water, red vinyl-padded chairs, plants that looked wilted even though they were plastic, and red and gold decorations left over from the Chinese New Year. The only thing that distinguished it was the oddly American-sounding name, the Lucky Duck, on a street full of Happy Families and Golden Pigs. Supposedly it was what someone had called Old Chou after he'd won the business in a card game. If there was anything lucky about the restaurant it was the duck—it was on the menu, but few people other than tourists asked for it. When they did, someone would have to run down the street to buy one from another restaurant that displayed whole roasted fowl and beef hearts that looked like they had been marinated in Mercurochrome.

Old Chou had called everyone over to fold napkins at the largest table, which could fit an extended family. Gao and Miguel were already laughing over some joke that was probably about women, something they didn't require knowing each other's language to understand. I could see the part on the top of Xiao Ru's head as she diligently folded napkins under Old Chou's gaze. I thought how interchangeable we all were, just another pair of hands to wash dishes, another pair of legs to carry them to a table. This would be true whether we worked here or at the restaurant next door. You could work at almost every restaurant in Chinatown and feel like you had worked in the same place all your life.

~ ~ ~

When I got to the park, I sat down on my regular bench and smoothed my hand over the cover of the book I had brought with me. It was a copy of *Anna Karenina* that I had bought one day from a sidewalk vendor in front of a university library. The binding was splintering apart and the pages were browned at the edges, but I liked thinking that it had belonged to a student, maybe even someone like me, reading it in a second language. I started reading slowly, my finger underlining the text, my mouth forming soundless shapes. Back in China, I would have taken out my dictionary the moment I encountered an unfamiliar word, but not here. Even if I couldn't understand half of what I read, I wanted to look like the other people sitting on the benches and reading, caught up in their worlds of perfect English.

I had read a Chinese translation of *Anna Karenina* at school, in Teacher Zhang's class. Teacher Zhang taught world literature, but he could have been teaching geometric equations for all we schoolgirls cared. Everyone in our class had a crush on him. We swooned over his hair, worn slightly longer than most local men's. We thought the curve of his lips was like that of a Taiwanese pop star's, his voice as melodious. When he stood in front of the class and recited poetry, it was easy to imagine him as one of those nobleman poets, with flowing hair and a beard, clad in a silk robe.

On the day we had been studying *Anna Karenina*, Teacher Zhang had asked us which couple we approved of more, Kitty and Levin or Anna and Vronsky. The overwhelming consensus was for Kitty and Levin.

"Why?" Teacher Zhang asked, arching a brow and sending the first row into a swoon.

The student who headed discussions in our political study class raised her hand. Teacher Zhang nodded in her direction. "Kitty and Levin show the proper collective spirit," she practically shouted. "Anna and Vronsky represent the bourgeois class."

"Do all of you think this?" Teacher Zhang swept us with a look that had as devastating an effect as his raised eyebrow. His gaze stopped at me, and I felt compelled to speak without raising my hand.

"Anna and Vronsky are the perfect couple," I said. "Theirs is a classic love story."

Teacher Zhang walked down the row of desks until he reached mine. He looked at me as if I were the only person in the room.

"But what about the fact that Anna leaves her husband and son for her lover?"

I hesitated. "It doesn't mean that she doesn't still love her son. She may still even love her husband, in a way. She just has to follow her heart. Otherwise she would regret not taking that chance for the rest of her life."

"And that's worth destroying the lives of everyone around her, including her own?"

My words were coming quicker now. "At least she took action about something she felt strongly about. At least she felt something. Right before she jumped in front of the train, she probably had never felt more alive in her life." I was feeling pretty reckless myself, saying these things.

"That's an interesting interpretation." Teacher Zhang turned to face the rest of the room. I was glad he did; I could barely breathe from his looking at me. "It seems that Miss Wu here has a different perspective. I would have thought that most of you shared it. I know how much girls your age care about romance"—embarrassed titters all around—"and what is more romantic than doomed passion?"

He smiled broadly at me when he said that, and I could sense my heart beating quicker and the color rising in my face. It was the first time Teacher Zhang had singled me out.

I was still feeling the heat of that memory when I looked up and saw, through the greenery of the park, two figures heading toward me: Lily and her mother, finally. Lily was wearing a red dress with white polka dots, and red ribbons trailed from her braids. Her mother wore a skirt that was the pale blue of the sky. Both of them barely looked at me as they sat down at their end of the bench. Then Lily went to the playground and her mother took out her own book.

I immediately turned my eyes back to the page open before me, but I could no longer concentrate on the world of nineteenth-century Russia. The words kept slipping out of my vision and toward the woman. After a while I noticed her looking at me.

"Which one is yours?" she asked in a friendly tone.

I followed the angle of her head to the playground. "Oh," I said, flushing. "I have no children." Then I realized what she meant. "I have no care—" That didn't sound right. "I don't take care of a child."

"I feel like I've seen you here before," she said.

"Yes." I looked at Lily.

"Oh right, that time we almost lost her mitten." The woman smiled, an American smile of even white teeth. "It was nice of you to be so concerned." Her gaze moved to the book in my lap. "Are you a foreign student?"

I wished that I could have said yes, but I shook my head. "I work in a restaurant in Chinatown." Before the words left my mouth I wondered if I should have lied and said I was indeed a student or a tourist. Old Chou told us that anyone who asked us questions was probably with immigration services.

But the woman just nodded. "I worked in a restaurant when I was a student. In *restaurants,* I should say. None of them ever kept me that long." She startled me with her strong laugh. "I broke a lot of dishes and added bills up wrong. But I remember making good tips, maybe forty dollars a night. That was a lot back then." The smile remained on her face, fixed but genuine.

I hesitantly returned a smile, wishing I could do it as easily as she could. For her it seemed as simple as breathing, while I had to force the corners of my mouth upward. Old Chou was always telling me to smile more at customers, but I found it hard to smile at people I didn't know, when there was nothing to be glad about. I tried to imagine this woman before me as a waitress, younger but with hair just as red, maybe twenty years ago.

"That tip money helped put me through five—no, six—years of college until they started letting me teach undergraduates," she continued.

"You are a teacher?"

"I was. I'm a curator now, at the Museum of Asian Art. Have you been there?"

I shook my head. I wasn't quite sure what a curator was.

"Oh, it's a wonderful place, at the risk of sounding like a walking PR machine. They just reopened their special exhibits wing, and they've got an amazing show right now with artists from Beijing. Very avant-garde, very political—they were banned in China, I believe. You should go sometime, I think you'd enjoy it."

I just nodded, confused by the various phrases she was tossing out, and taken aback that in the space of a few minutes she seemed to know me so well that she could tell what I liked.

"I'm sorry," the woman said. "I haven't introduced myself. I'm Jane Templeton."

"Like the street?" I said.

She looked at me for a moment, confused, and then her eyes lit with recognition. "Yes, like Jane Street."

"My name is Hua." I pronounced it flatly, knowing that Americans couldn't grasp the tones that gave every Chinese character a different meaning.

"Hua." Jane repeated the word with precision. "What a pretty name. Is it the character for flower?"

Surprised and pleased that she knew that much, I said, "Yes, it is."

"Lily," and Jane looked fondly upon her daughter, "originally had a name that I couldn't pronounce. Her nickname at the orphanage was Li Li, so we decided to call her Lily."

"It is a nice name."

"Well, I thought it would be best to keep it short, since her last name is Templeton-Walker. Walker is my husband's last name."

We both looked toward Lily, who was playing with a doll. After a while she came over and leaned against her mother's knee, staring at me with wide eyes.

"Remember Hua?" Jane said to her. "We would have lost your mitten if it wasn't for her."

Lily just continued to stare at me, her lower lip pushed out.

"Why don't you show Hua your doll?"

Reluctantly she held it up, a plastic, chubby-cheeked doll with blond hair and blue eyes.

Jane gave an embarrassed wave of her hand. "I know dolls like this aren't the best thing for her to play with, but dolls that look, well, Asian, are hard to come by. What toys do children have in China?"

"There are dolls like this." On impulse I took the doll from Lily and saw, under its hairline, the raised words Made in China. I showed this to Jane, who laughed.

"I know, but what kind of traditional toys would children play with? What did you play with?"

I tried to think back to those days. I could remember my grandmother standing in front of our door, calling me in. I could remember tossing rocks at a stray dog and chasing it down the street. Going down by the river to collect pebbles or bits of broken glass worn smooth by the waves. Climbing trees to look over other people's walls and throwing mud on their clean laundry, then running away. These were not things I could recommend.

Then an image came into my head: a colored-pencil sketch from a schoolbook I'd had as a child, of children flying kites in a park. "Kites," I finally said. "We played with kites." I had never seen a park like that before in my life, a wide expanse of grass ringed by trees and some tall buildings, with a cloudless blue sky overhead. For some reason I thought it might be in America.

"Kites." Jane sounded charmed by the idea. "We could go to Central Park to fly kites. Or maybe wait until the summer when we go to the country."

The bizarre image of Jane and Lily trudging through a field, while peasants and their oxen stopped to stare, flashed into my head.

Lily extended one finger toward the doll I was still holding. "Mine," she said, her face screwed into a frown. Before I could react, she grabbed it away from me.

"Lily, Lily." Jane clucked her tongue. "Don't be so greedy. She's at that stage where she hates to share. Maybe it comes from not having a sibling."

I felt bold enough to ask, "What does it mean, sibling?"

"Brother or sister. She's an only child."

"I am also," I said. "But many children in China are like this. It's the policy."

Jane nodded. "Of course, the One Child Policy. Unfortunate but necessary. And without it, Lily probably wouldn't be here. She'd be with her real mother and father, and with who knows how many brothers and sisters. There's no way of knowing." She looked at me. "Are your parents back in China?"

"My parents"—I tried to remember the polite term for it—
"passed away."

"I'm so sorry." Jane's voice lowered with sympathy. "How
old were you when you lost them?"

"Three years old. I lived with my grandmother."

"She must be a very strong woman."

"Yes."

For some reason, maybe the mention of my grandmother,
maybe the compassion in Jane's voice, my vision clouded
with tears. I forced myself to stare at the playground to re-
gain control.

Jane seemed to sense my sadness and she also looked away.
Lily, however, banged the doll against the bench. "Mommy,
the swings," she said. She spoke clearly, insistently.

Jane glanced at her watch and sighed. "Sorry, baby, maybe
next time—it's getting late. I try to take Lily here every day,
even if it's just for a short time," she explained to me as she
began gathering up her things. "But she's had a cold for the
past few weeks and I've been busy, so we haven't been out in
a while."

Lily caught on to what her mother was doing and said,
"No!"

"Now, Lily—"

Lily threw herself down on the ground and began wailing.
She kicked and flailed and slammed the doll in the dirt. I had
never seen a child throw a tantrum like that before.

"I don't know what's gotten into her," Jane said.

She opened the stroller and tried to wrestle her daughter
into it. I half stood, wanting to help but not knowing what to
do. Lily's sharp little hands and feet were flying everywhere.
Finally she sat quietly, with an occasional hiccup, tears streak-
ing her face. She was still clutching the doll.

"There now," Jane said. "I think we need to take a nap when we get home and then everything will be okay." To me she added, "It was very nice to meet you, Hua."

"Very nice to meet you," I echoed.

Jane peered down into the stroller. "Won't you say good-bye to Hua, Lily?"

Lily remained silent.

"Say good-bye to Hua, Lily."

Lily threw the doll in my direction. It fell short and the head separated from the body. It rolled a few inches away on the ground, the glassy eyes staring up into the sky. For a moment we all stared at it, dumbfounded. Then the wailing started again, furiously.

"Lily!" Jane gasped. "That was a very bad thing to do!"

I picked up the pieces of the doll and handed them to Jane. She stuffed them into her bag with a distracted "thank you" and then moved off. I watched them leave the playground as the sound of Lily's wailing floated away beneath the new spring leaves.

Part II

Chapter Four

A shadow passed over the page of *Anna Karenina*.

"You're getting through that book quickly," a voice said.

I looked up to see Jane and Lily standing before me. "It is not too hard," I said. "Hello, Lily."

Lily smiled from behind her mother's arm, still bashful around me even though I had been seeing her and Jane in the park for a few weeks now. I always got to the bench before they did and would wait nervously for their appearance at the gate. Jane would seem preoccupied when she arrived, but she would relax as we talked, her face and body falling softly into place. Mostly Jane talked about herself and asked me questions, about my grandmother, what growing up in Fuzhou had been like. The only thing I was reluctant to talk about was my present life. I didn't want her to think of me as a waitress she might find if she walked into any restaurant in Chinatown.

Now I took out the second book I had brought with me, an atlas of China. I had found it in a used-book store and spent part of my weekly wages on it, money I should have sent back to my grandmother. The week before, Jane had mentioned that Lily had come from an orphanage in a town in Jiangxi Province, which was next to Fujian Province where I had grown up. From what I knew, the people who lived in Jiangxi were very poor, especially compared to their neighbors —the *fu* in Fujian meant wealth. I wanted to see if Jane and I could find Lily's hometown on a map.

With Lily sitting next to Jane and leaning over her lap to look, I opened the book to the right map. Jiangxi Province was shaped like a human heart, with the left and right sections separated by a lake.

"The place was called Liping, in the southeast," Jane recalled.

I searched until I found the name beneath a dot that indicated a small town. "This is Liping," I said. "This is where Lily is from."

Jane turned her head to look at where my finger pointed. "Or the closest we can get, I guess. Lily was actually found on the doorstep of the local temple outside of town. The people at the orphanage thought she was from one of the smaller villages to the north." She traced the line of a road that wove away from the town through the blue-green shading that meant mountains. "The first picture we saw of her had been taken right after she'd arrived at the orphanage. It was a bad picture all right, her hair was sticking straight up and she was crying. She hardly looked human—more like a little wild animal or something." Jane placed her hand on top of Lily's head. "But that was the picture we fell in love with. She was around two months old and we had to wait nine more months before we could go get her. And even then we weren't allowed to go to the town where the orphanage was. We had to wait for her to be brought to us in Guangzhou."

I flipped through the pages to a map of Guangdong Province, hundreds of miles to the south, where the modern city of Guangzhou lay.

"Lily and her caretaker from the orphanage had to take a bus because no trains went to Liping, it was so remote. We sat in that hotel in Guangzhou for a week waiting for the bus to arrive because it kept getting delayed by mud slides and flat tires. It would have been easier for us to have gone out there ourselves, but those were the rules."

"Maybe it is too hard for you to see," I suggested.

"Oh, I know the living conditions in those places can be awful. But it would have been nice to have had some idea of what her hometown was like. Even to meet someone who could have been from her family."

"Maybe she has no family," I said. "If she has relatives, they will take care of her. It is their family obligation."

"Well, lucky for us then, the orphanage didn't look hard enough."

Or, more likely, I thought, there was a good reason no one had come forth to claim Lily. Her mother might have been young and unmarried, or her father married to someone else, or she was the second child, or she was the first daughter. There must be some kind of shame attached to her that no one would ever know, least of all her new parents. She had no background, no history, except for what was here in her new home.

"You must think it's ridiculous that we went through all that trouble and expense to adopt a child in China," Jane said. "Most of the Chinese people we met in Guangzhou seemed to think so. We'd walk down the street and people would stare or smile, but not in a good way. More like they thought we were crazy."

"No," I said. "I don't think that."

"I'm relieved to hear it."

I didn't say any more. I didn't know if I had the words to explain what I was thinking anyway. In some respects it was that simple: Lily needed parents and Jane and her husband needed a child. But foreigners were forever meddling in business that wasn't theirs, taking things that didn't belong to them. From the hill where my grandmother lived in Fuzhou, you could see various church spires: the Roman Catholic church built by the Germans, the Protestant church built by the British, the religious school started by American missionaries. No one had asked them to go there and save anybody.

"I mean, we could have tried to adopt a child here in America," Jane continued, "but there's always the chance that the birth mother will try to take the baby back. That's not going to happen with a Chinese baby. And I guess we could have adopted from another country—some friends of ours adopted from Romania seven years ago—but I guess I've always felt a connection with China, with my work at the museum and everything."

"It is fate," I said.

A curious look crossed Jane's face. "Maybe it is. No one's ever said that to me before. Probably because it sounds a little, you know, sentimental."

I looked down at my hands gripping the edge of the book. My grandmother was a great believer in fate. It was perhaps the only thing that kept her from despair throughout all the unfortunate things that had happened to our family.

Jane touched my hand. "I'm sorry, it was a nice thing, what you said. A lot of people aren't so kind about it. They think that if you can't have children the natural way, you shouldn't have them at all. But I wasn't all that young when I met my husband, and it took me a long time to realize I wanted a child. I came to New York after college, and before I knew it, twenty years had passed in a flash."

I must have looked as if I didn't believe her, because she added, "You'll see. These first months must seem like ages to you, but once you get used to it, you won't know where the years went. There's just too much to do here, too much to soak up. It leaves room for nothing else."

I didn't think that could happen to me as easily as it had happened to her, that my days would ever hold anything other than restaurant work and Chinatown. "But we are different," I pointed out.

"Not so much as you would think." Jane gave a wry laugh. "I grew up in the Midwest. If you ever go there, you'll see that it's like another country. I went to a small college an hour from my hometown, so coming to New York was my first time away from home." She shook her head. "I didn't think I'd made the right decision when I got here. The first place I lived was awful. I shared an apartment with an actress and a singer, and it sure got noisy."

I thought of the other people in my boardinghouse and agreed. "The place where I live is noisy, too."

"You see? Everyone starts out that way. Well, I was miserable at first. I missed my family and friends and open spaces. Then there was this one magical night—I'd gotten a cheap standing-room ticket to the Metropolitan Opera. I had only heard opera before on the radio at home, on the weekend when they'd broadcast performances from New York. But this time I actually saw and heard it in real life. I remember standing on the steps of the Met afterward, awestruck, like I was in a dream. It was starting to snow, and all these elderly couples who'd had expensive seats were rushing into taxis around me, and I just stood there. I ended up walking home forty blocks in the snow, trying to make that evening last."

She stopped, and in that moment I could see her, a young woman in a thin coat, not caring that her hair was covered with snow.

"So," Jane said, "don't think things won't change."

I looked around at the playground adrift with tiny, pale yellow blossoms that had floated down from the trees, so different from the icy gray landscape I had first seen a few months ago, then back to Jane. She was frowning down at her watch.

"Great," she said, but she didn't sound pleased. "Are you going to be here for a while?"

I nodded.

"Do you think you could watch Lily for me? I need to run to the post office and certify a letter before it closes. It's right down the street. I won't be more than fifteen minutes, I promise." Jane was already rising to her feet and hitching her bag up on her shoulder.

"Yes, okay," I said before I could think about it. I'm not sure what I could have said otherwise.

"Thanks. Stay with Hua now," Jane told Lily. "Mommy will be right back." She sped off faster than I thought would have been possible in her high-heeled shoes.

I looked sideways at Lily, and she seemed to look doubtfully back at me. I had no idea what watching a child meant, despite all the hours I had spent watching the children on the playground. Most of the nannies seemed able to do at least two things at once, keeping one eye on their charges and the other on their knitting or talking. I hoped Lily wouldn't cry at being left alone with a stranger, but after another long look at me, she didn't seem to mind. I guess she was used to being left with other people. We looked through the rest of the maps together, and I let Lily turn the pages as fast as she wanted until they were a sweep of color: the pale green of the Inner Mongolian grasslands, the dark blue-green of the southwestern border with the Himalayas, the yellows and oranges of the deserts in the northwest, places neither of us had ever seen.

Minutes passed, and I tried to imagine where Jane was at the post office. She must be standing in line. Only five more people now and she'd reach a window, and then she'd be on her way back. Too bad my thoughts couldn't make the line move any faster. My mind wandered further, to the post office back home in Fuzhou; it had counters with pots of paste that looked like thick mucus which was used to stick stamps on letters. No one stood in line there. You just crowded up against the open window and the first person who shoved his letter through got it taken care of. And usually there would be a little old man or woman who would sneak under your arm at the last minute, and you had to let them go ahead out of respect for the elderly.

A child's sharp and sudden cry startled me from my thoughts. I looked around, hoping that Lily hadn't hurt herself while I was daydreaming. It seemed to have come from another child, a little boy who had fallen off one of the swings. Then I saw Lily on the other side of the playground next to a long, twisty, silver snake of a slide. Her foot was posed on the bottom rung of the ladder that led up to the top.

I rushed over before she could get her other foot off the ground.

"This is too high for you," I said in Chinese. She looked at me, uncomprehending. I repeated it in English, adding what I'd heard other nannies say, often without success: "Get down *now.*"

"No," she said. Apparently this was her favorite word with everyone, not just her mother.

I glimpsed a second slide that sloped gently to the ground from a series of three or four steps, made for younger children.

"You can go on that one," I told her, pointing.

She pulled me over to the baby slide. I stood next to the steps as she climbed, keeping one hand at her back without touching it, not because I thought I could catch her if she fell but just because *I* felt safer that way. I looked around the park to see if Jane had appeared. Maybe she didn't think Lily was old enough to go on the slide by herself. Would she scold me if she found out?

"Watch me!" Lily had reached the top of the slide. She sat down, her legs sticking out like her braids. As I had seen the other nannies do, I went around to the bottom of the slide and crouched in the sand, my arms outstretched to catch her. She scooted down the slide and landed in my arms. She held on to me so tightly that I couldn't have dropped her even if I'd tried. Then she wriggled out of my grasp and ran to climb the steps to the slide again.

On her fifth or sixth time down the slide, I caught a glimpse of Jane back from the post office, sitting on our bench. I had no idea how long she had been there, simply watching us. When she saw me glance at her, she waved and I lifted a hand in response. Lily didn't seem to notice so I let her continue playing, knowing that her mother approved.

I was glad, though, when Jane came over to us. My knees hurt from crouching at the end of the slide, and I could feel sand gritting in my shoes. Lily ran to her mother. For a moment I missed that feeling of her small clinging arms, as if I were the only person who could possibly protect her.

"Did you have a good time playing with Hua?" Jane asked Lily, kneeling and smoothing back the hair that had come loose from her braids.

Lily nodded but without looking at me. Now that her mother was around, it wasn't so important to her that I was there.

"Thank you for watching her," Jane said to me. "You did a very good job. And she likes you very much, I can tell. Really, thank you."

I felt like I had just passed an important test. I tried to think of the right English phrase to use in response, the proper level of informality for this situation. "It was nothing."

~ ~ ~

Jane's errand had reminded me that I was supposed to go to the post office and send a letter to my grandmother, making sure she had received the money I had wired earlier that month. So the next day, between the noon and evening shift at work, I asked if I could take some time off. Gao was in charge because Old Chou was at Off-Track Betting for the afternoon—if his wife called we were supposed to say he was in the storeroom taking a nap. I never understood why Old Chou gave Gao that authority, even if Gao had worked there the longest. Although he had previously lived in Guangzhou, Gao was originally from Sichuan Province, which, my grandmother would have said, meant he had a fiery temper from the spicy food he ate growing up. I didn't always believe my grandmother when she said things like that. She said the same thing about the local tofu seller who was also from Sichuan, using it as an excuse to not buy tofu from him. She could have just said that she didn't like him, which was the truth. But no, she couldn't admit she disliked anyone, so instead the tofu seller had a fiery temper.

But I have to say, Gao fit that description. If he wasn't openly angry about something, he was sulking, which was worse. He seemed to feel that everyone was conspiring against him, whether it was somebody neglecting to mop the floor under his section of the counter or misplacing his favorite chopping knife. After Li injured his finger and had to take a week off, Gao said that Li had done it on purpose just to make more work for him. Li had returned by now, a bandage still on his index finger. He enjoyed pulling back the bandage and showing us the fresh scar tissue, which was the pale pink of a newborn mouse. Xiao Ru always screamed when he did this.

"Okay," Gao said when I told him what I needed to do. "But come right back. Don't go off to pay a bill. Don't stop at the market." He turned to the counter and then whirled back. "Don't go visiting friends."

It galled me that Gao spoke to us that way. Old Chou I could understand and tolerate, as he was our boss, but Gao was just a chicken pretending to be a rooster. "Don't worry, I have no friends to visit," I told him and left.

As I passed Off-Track Betting, I looked in the window to see if I could spot Old Chou. But all I saw behind the grimy glass was a knot of faceless men clutching tickets, looking up at the television monitors. They were probably either unemployed or, like Old Chou, new store owners too impatient to wait for their businesses to succeed. This or the lottery was the only real way to get rich quick.

The post office on Doyers Street was quiet and orderly. I stood at the end of the line and imagined I was Jane from the other day, tall in my high heels, calm, with my purse on my arm. Then I noticed, a few people ahead, a woman who was looking back at me. It didn't take me long to place her.

This woman had been part of the group of seven people who had made the journey from Fuzhou to New York with me. We'd gone from Fuzhou to Shenzhen by bus, crossed the border into Hong Kong on foot, and then flown to Bangkok with illegal travel documents. There we'd joined a larger group of Taiwanese tourists bound for the United States. None of us mainland Chinese talked to each other much, as if we were afraid of giving something away. But because this woman and I were the only two females in our group, we'd shared a room during the trip. After a while we'd gotten to know each other a little. She'd wanted me to call her by her English name, Sally.

When I had first seen Sally back in Fuzhou, I knew she wasn't from the city. She was only a few years older than me, but her round face was lined from the sun and her hands were chapped. When we were in Shenzhen she looked wide-eyed at everything, as though she had never been in a big city before. But in the Chinatown post office, we looked more like each other than I'd thought, especially the way we kept our eyes on the ground and our shoulders hunched, as if fearing the world would swallow us at any moment. To everyone else here, we looked like newly arrived immigrants.

At first Sally looked surprised to see me, then frightened, then eager to talk. She motioned for me to step out of the line and join her on the side. When I did, she drew my arm into hers like we were friends.

"How are you, Hua?" she whispered. "Are you doing well?"

"I've found a job and a place to live," I replied vaguely. "You?"

She hesitated. "Me, too. My job's not the best, but I get good tips." She expelled a breath and confided, indicating our surroundings, "I don't like being in a government office."

I didn't think there was anything for her to be afraid of. Even though the post office had the symbols of eagles and flags everywhere, like customs at the airport, the postal workers were all Chinese.

"I keep thinking someone will recognize me and arrest me," she said. Then she looked at me meaningfully. "Or you."

When we had arrived at the airport in New York, we'd stood patiently in line, buried within the group of Taiwanese tourists, to get our documents checked. Our guide—an oily man who insisted on our calling him *da ge,* or "big brother"—had already passed through and was watching to make sure we didn't mess up. There was nothing we could do but try to look as if we fit in. Sally was behind me and I could feel each of her nervous breaths.

I passed through, and then she passed through, but before our guide could join us a man interceded. He didn't look particularly official except that he was wearing a blue suit and was as broad as a brick wall. He put his hand on Sally's arm and asked both of us to step aside. My body tingled with fear from head to foot, and Sally looked like she would have collapsed if the man hadn't been holding her up. This man was the first real American we had encountered thus far, and he did not make a good impression. He towered over us, and his hand on Sally's arm looked like a large piece of freckled meat. His neck rose large and dark pink from his shirt collar, and above that his face showed no expression, his eyes hard.

He asked us to provide our documents again.

What is he saying? Sally's eyes asked me. I pulled out my passport and hoped she would follow my example.

As the customs official looked through our documents, I knew I had to be the one to say something, as Sally hardly knew any English. I looked over my shoulder to where the other people from our group were standing, having passed through safely, huddled around our guide like frightened geese. Our guide gave me a look and I remembered what he had coached us to say if we were caught in this situation.

"Sir," I said, too loud.

The customs official's head snapped up and he looked surprised to hear me speak so clearly.

"I am pregnant, but I already have one child at home." My voice shook at the lie and I steadied it. "If I go back, the Chinese government will kill the child in my belly."

I managed to look into the official's eyes without wavering, and they seemed to expand before me with confusion.

"Her, too?" he said, indicating Sally. She looked anxiously from him to me and back again, not understanding what was going on.

"For her, too."

The official's eyes held mine for a long moment. Then he handed back our travel documents. "Okay," he said. "You can both go."

When we reached our group, Sally was practically weeping from relief. I held on to her, my own legs weak, and told our guide what had happened. He looked smug that his tactic had worked. He had told us that if we said we were pregnant and fleeing from the Chinese government's One Child Policy, the American officials might be lenient. They were too good of Christians to make us go back.

Remembering this now in the Chinatown post office, I had to laugh. "We fooled them that time."

Sally looked more at ease. "Yes, we did." She added, "You're lucky your relatives came to get you at the airport afterward."

After our ordeal, we'd gone into the waiting room where a Chinese couple in their early sixties asked for me. They spoke briefly to the guide—something about a phone call back to Fuzhou to tell my grandmother that I had arrived safely, and that the full balance had been paid—and I had been released into their care. I hadn't given a thought to what everyone else in my group had done after I had left them.

"Why, what happened?" I asked.

"The guide took us to this house somewhere outside the city. A safe house, he called it. We waited in a basement for three days before we were allowed to leave. Two men watched us the whole time, even if you had to use the bathroom."

"Why did they treat you like that?" During our trip, we had been treated well, like we were real tourists on our way to America. True, when we were in the intermediary cities we weren't allowed to leave our rooms, but we were told that it was safer for us that way, that we couldn't afford being caught with our fake documents. We couldn't be caught with them in America either; the guide had taken them away from us in the waiting room.

Sally's eyes widened. "You don't know? We had to stay there if we owed money. Our transportation fees. Your relatives must be rich if you could go with them. If we even stepped outside of the house we would have been beaten. People have gotten killed for less."

I took a deep breath. I guessed I was lucky indeed. "But you got out okay."

Sally shrugged. "I have a cousin who lives here and was supposed to be my sponsor, but he went back on his word. I still owe the snakeheads money. But they got me my job. I make much more here than I would have back home, no matter what I did. Last year I was planning to go find work in Hong Kong, but it was a much better idea to come to America."

"So you like it here?"

"It's more exciting than back home. But I miss it sometimes."

"Me, too," I admitted.

Sally giggled, covering her mouth with her hand. "Of course, I can't tell anyone back home what I do here. Especially my mother. I'd be so ashamed."

When she said that, I understood what Sally did for a living. My eyes moved from her arms, one still linked in mine, to her hands, which I had noticed were so rough when I'd first met her back in China. Now her nails ended in perfectly manicured half-circles. But I knew that she had to do more with those hands than just give a massage to get those good tips she'd mentioned earlier. I found myself starting to back away from her, her touch suddenly unbearable.

"Are you all right?" she asked.

"Yes," I lied. "I just forgot something." At the same time I pushed the letter I had intended to post further into my pocket.

"See you again," Sally called after me, but I had already turned my back on her.

By the time I got back to the restaurant I was in a foul mood. I was angry at myself for the way I had treated Sally and that I hadn't posted my letter. Gao wasn't pleased either.

"Where were you?" he demanded, knife upraised. "You've been gone almost half an hour. Did you stop to count all the cars that passed you in the street?"

"Asshole," I muttered under my breath in English, using a word that I had heard a young woman use when a delivery boy's bicycle had splashed mud on her.

Gao had heard it before, too. "What did you say?"

The other workers had stopped what they were doing and were watching us now. I saw an amused look on Li's face, Xiao Ru's startled eyes.

"Just because Old Chou left you in charge," I said, "doesn't mean you're the boss."

Gao was so close to me that I could smell the crisp greenness of just-cut scallions on his knife. "You're so proud just because you can speak English better than anyone else here. But I've been in this country longer than you. Let's see if you can last a year."

"I can," I said. "I will."

Although my voice was steady, my eyes couldn't help flicking toward the knife Gao still held in his hand. He noticed it, too, and lowered it, a grudging smile crossing his face. "Maybe you will, then."

I regarded him warily, unsure of his change in mood. Then I saw Old Chou come in from the dining room. Gao immediately shrank back to his workstation.

"What's going on here?" Old Chou asked, clapping his hands. "Work! Work!" But he was grinning; he must have had a good day at the races.

As everyone turned back to their jobs, Xiao Ru tugged on my sleeve and whispered to me, "What was that English word you called Gao? I want to learn it."

~ ～ ~

I continued to think of Sally in the following days, as I walked the few short blocks from the boardinghouse to work and back, while I was waiting for orders and clearing tables. As much as I hated my job in the restaurant, I knew there were worse things

I could be doing. I was fortunate that I had relatives here in America that I could turn to if something went wrong, otherwise I could have ended up in Sally's situation. When I had first seen Sally back in China, knowing that she had come from the countryside, I had been firmly convinced that we had been heading toward different fates in America, even though we were taking the same route to get there. But once we arrived, it was as if passing through customs at the airport had completely erased our identities and our pasts. We were made the same, and we were on our own.

When I looked around at the other workers in the restaurant, I thought of how little I knew about them. I knew the places in China they had come from, but not what their lives had been like there. I didn't know what they did when they weren't at work, or what they hoped their lives would become. And they probably knew as little about me. But none of my coworkers had the park and the visits with Jane and Lily. Those things set me apart from them.

The following week, toward the end of an afternoon in the park, Jane turned to me with a serious look on her face. I instantly thought the worst, that she was going to tell me that for some reason she and Lily weren't going to come to the park anymore.

Instead, Jane said, "I have another favor to ask of you, Hua. My husband and I have an important dinner to go to Saturday night and our regular babysitter can't come. Would you be able to watch Lily for us?"

"Where?"

"Why, in our house."

I sat there in stunned silence. I couldn't believe that Jane would ask me, a virtual stranger, inside of her own house.

Jane misinterpreted my silence. "We'd pay you, of course. We'd be gone maybe five or six hours. Would this be a problem where you work?"

I thought quickly. There must be something I could tell Old Chou to get that evening off. "No," I said. "No problem."

"Wonderful. I'll write down directions to our apartment for you. Actually, why don't you walk back with me and Lily now? It's just a few blocks away. That is, if you have the time."

So we walked down the street, Jane pushing the stroller with Lily, and me following a little behind. We stopped in front of one of the buildings I had admired when I first discovered the park. The flowers in the window boxes of the first-floor apartment bloomed red and white against the brown stone, and green vines clustered thickly around the pillars that framed the entrance.

"We're on the second floor, apartment B," Jane said. She showed me TEMPLETON/WALKER in the list of names outside the front door. "When you arrive, press the buzzer and I'll let you in." Then she wrote the address on a piece of paper, along with a telephone number. "That's our number. Give me a call if you can't come on Saturday. Otherwise, we'll see you at six."

I nodded. We said good-bye, and I watched Jane and Lily pass through the front door. Then it swung closed and all I could see in the glass panes was my own reflection and the row of brownstones on the other side of the street.

Chapter Five

On Saturday evening I stood in front of the Templeton-Walkers' apartment building. Although it was six o'clock, sunlight spread across the Hudson River, between the buildings, and down the street.

I had arrived early, although I had gone home from the restaurant first to change my clothes, convinced that the smell of cooking oil wafted from my pores. It hadn't taken me long to convince Old Chou to let me off from work. I had cornered him in the storeroom where he did the bills, and told him that I needed to stay with my sick aunt in New Jersey. Old Chou had been too involved with adding up receipts to question me. He muttered that it was a good thing he had a relative visiting from China who could help out and waved me from the room.

Before I could press the buzzer for 2B, the door to the building swung open and a huge dog strained down the steps. I jumped back as a long red leash followed the dog, which, in turn, was followed by a middle-aged man.

"Don't worry," the man said as the dog sniffed me. "He's friendly."

I nodded as I shrunk back against the side of the building, wondering if the dog could tell that I was a stranger. But the man held the door open for me as if I lived there and I smiled my thanks, startled by this polite gesture. In the cool, dim light of the lobby, I could see a strip of carpet that led up the hallway. The floor on either side was so polished it looked like the surface of a lake. On the second floor I pressed a doorbell. I heard the sound of flying feet and a child's voice calling, "Ria! Ria!"

Jane opened the door; Lily's face peeked out at her side. At the first sight of me Lily scowled, turned, and ran away down the hall.

"Please don't mind her, Hua. She's expecting her usual babysitter, Margarita," Jane said. "Come on in. I didn't hear you ring downstairs. That's the trouble with old buildings like these, something is always broken. Plus what I wouldn't give to have a doorman. . . ."

I followed Jane's voice down the narrow hall and into the living room. A dark plush rug stretched from the fireplace and television at one end to a sofa at the other, its intricate pattern mostly obscured by toys. Jane led me quickly through the rest of the apartment: her and Richard's room, Lily's room, a dining room with a chandelier, a kitchen gleaming with stainless steel. Back in the living room, Lily stood in the center of the rug, watching me with wary eyes.

"Well," Jane said, "I still need to get ready. Richard should be home any minute. Lily, why don't you show Hua your favorite toy?" She touched my shoulder as she passed me. "I'll be right back."

I hadn't expected to be left alone with Lily so soon. She looked at me with her usual stern gaze, but she stayed in the room. I picked up a stuffed bunny.

"Is this your favorite toy?" I asked.

Lily shook her head.

I chose a red telephone with a smiling face for a dial. "This one?"

"No, this one!" Lily showed me a doll that was different from the one she'd broken a few weeks ago in the park. This one had pink hair and smelled like someone's idea of strawberries.

"She's very pretty," I said, pretending to admire the doll's rosy-cheeked face and blank stare.

Lily considered the doll and threw it on the ground. "No, this one!" she said, and brought me a dirty yellow bear with a string coming out of its back. She yanked the string so that the bear squeaked something and then she tossed it aside.

As a pile of discarded toys grew by my feet, I examined my surroundings. Lining the walls were more books than I had ever seen before in one room, many of them art books too large to fit upright so they were stacked on their sides. A Chinese brush painting hung above the fireplace, depicting a lone temple rising from a cloud bed. Below it on the mantelpiece stood a collection of antique snuff bottles. Their oval green-and-amber surfaces were painted with the images of courtesans combing their hair or holding fans that resembled the wings of butterflies.

The floorboards groaned and a large black cat ambled into the room. It leapt up on the sofa and regarded me critically with gold-flecked eyes. Then I heard footsteps approach, and a man whom I supposed was Jane's husband entered. He was large and seemed to be very brown, from his shoes and his suit to his hair, which was crinkled with gray. Lily ran to him.

"Hello," he said to me, offering his hand as Lily hung on to his arm. "You must be Hua. I'm Richard, the father of this little spider monkey." He swung Lily up to his shoulder and she screamed with laughter.

"And that's Otello sitting next to you," Jane said from the doorway. She had changed into a simple black dress and high heels, and her red hair was swept up. I glanced at the cat, who blinked at me. "So I guess you've met the whole family now. Can you come with me into the kitchen? I have a few things to go over before we leave."

I sat down at a spotless countertop as Jane showed me a list of numbers to call in case of an emergency: her's and Richard's cell phones, Lily's pediatrician, a twenty-four-hour vet, the next-door neighbor, the superintendent downstairs, the hospital, the fire department, the police.

"Lily's had her dinner already, but feel free to take whatever you want." Jane gestured toward the fridge. "Later in the evening you can heat up a bottle for her in the microwave. Just make sure it's cool enough before you give it to her. We're trying to start potty training but for now, her diapers and everything else you'll need are in her room. Try to put her to bed in a couple of hours, but if she doesn't want to go to sleep, don't force her. Read to her, and if that doesn't work, put on a video. Anything with animals that talk, she likes."

I nodded, trying to keep up with her list of instructions.

"Oh, and when you put her to bed, leave the bathroom light on and her door partway open so that she has a night light. Do you have any questions?"

I shook my head. I could hear shouts of laughter from the living room.

"She likes her father," I said aloud, thinking how I had never really considered Lily as having a father; in the park it was just her and Jane.

"Lily was very scared of Richard in the beginning," Jane said. "She'd cry and wouldn't let him touch her. They thought it was because she hadn't seen a lot of men before, since all of the caretakers at the orphanage were women. So to get her more used to him, he'd be the one to get up and go to her when she cried at night. That arrangement suited me fine."

"What is your husband's work?"

"He's a theater critic." Jane leaned in closer over the counter-top as if sharing a secret. "Actually, before I met him, he wrote plays. Then he had a year of bad reviews, got depressed, and tried to make himself feel better by reviewing other people's plays. Turned out it was much easier to write a bad review than to receive one, and he's been doing that ever since. We're going to the opening of a show tonight. It's not really my kind of thing, but I have to be supportive." She shrugged. "At least it gives one an opportunity to dress up."

"You look very nice," I ventured to say, but Jane had turned to fix the list of emergency numbers on the refrigerator door and seemed not to hear me.

In the living room Lily was sitting on the sofa watching television. But when her parents started to leave, she ran to Jane and clung to the back of her black satin evening coat.

"Don't worry," Jane said. "We'll be back in no time. Why, sweetie, we go out a lot of weekends! This one's no different. Call us if anything comes up," she said to me. "We'll be back around eleven."

Richard nodded at me, his hand underneath Jane's arm, and then they were gone.

I eyed Lily, expecting the tears to come. But she just rocked from one foot to the other, twisting a corner of her skirt in her hands. She looked as if she knew that not only was I not her regular babysitter but I was no kind of babysitter at all. Then she turned and left the room. I had the uncomfortable feeling that I had just lost some kind of contest.

I stayed still for a moment, debating whether I should go see what Lily was up to. Of course I couldn't be following her everywhere she went in the house for the rest of the night. But I was beginning to mistrust the silence in the room following Lily's departure. Then I heard a crash.

Dirt spilled across the hall from a large potted plant in a vase that now lay on its side. Lily stood a few feet away from it, her eyes large. She watched me right the vase and scoop the dirt back in. When I was finished, I stood up and said in my best Jane voice, "Lily! That was a very bad thing to do!"

As her face crumpled I saw that Lily had truly been frightened by what had happened. She hadn't meant to make the vase come crashing down; she had probably just wanted to see what was inside. I stopped myself from imagining what could have happened if she hadn't jumped back fast enough.

"It's all right," I said, lowering my voice. I patted her on the head awkwardly, as if she were the cat. "Let's go into the other room and watch television, okay?"

She obediently followed me back into the living room. After a few minutes I figured out that we weren't watching a television program but a DVD Richard must have put on before he and Jane had left. It was a cartoon involving animals that were not their proper colors—a red bear, a green giraffe, and a blue lion.

At one point I asked Lily, "What is this?"

She turned to me with a finger over her lips and shushed me.

It soon appeared that Lily would be content to watch television for the rest of the evening, so I left her there and went to explore the rest of the apartment.

Lily's room was very clearly a little girl's room, with flowered wallpaper and lace-trimmed pillows and more dolls. The doll Lily had broken in the park would never be missed among all these others with blond hair or brown hair, blue eyes or green eyes. I imagined what the room must have looked like right before Lily had arrived. Jane would have prepared for months, making sure the sheets were smooth enough, the curtains the right thickness to block the light. When the adoption agency called to tell her that the process was taking longer than expected, she'd stand in the middle of the baby's room and the emptiness would mock her. Then she was finally able to bring Lily home, and on the first day she would have seen that the toys she'd bought were for a newborn, not a child who was already almost a year old.

Down the hall was Jane and Richard's room, which had more books and a bed so wide I suspected that two people lying in it could reach toward each other in the middle of the night without touching. I lay down on the bed and looked toward the window where the shadow of a tree branch crossed the pane. It must be what Jane saw before she went to sleep at night and the first thing she saw in the morning.

I opened the closet and saw that one side was clearly Richard's with its uniform shades of brown and gray. On the other side I could identify items that Jane had worn to the park. The gleam of something sleek and white caught the corner of my eye. It was the cream-colored coat Jane had worn when I first saw her and Lily, relegated to the back of the closet with the changing seasons. I wrestled the coat from its hanger and put it on, the lining cool against my skin. I snuggled back into the collar, thinking it was the softest thing I had ever felt. It was too large for me, but when I looked at myself in the mirror, I felt transformed. If I were walking down the street wearing this coat, someone would stop to look at me.

Still wearing the coat, I sat down at a vanity table. It was as if I could see the pattern of Jane's thoughts in the things scattered across its surface: several lipsticks that had been rejected because they were too bright, a pair of earrings she'd decided were too flashy. I held a single earring up to my unpierced ear, felt it brush against my neck. I opened a compact and dusted some powder onto my face. Instantly my complexion, which my grandmother always said was too brown, shimmered like pearl. I picked a lipstick and painted a precise, red mouth. I dabbed on some of Jane's perfume so it left a whisper of scent. When I was done, I lifted my chin and turned my head so that the light reflected from the mirror ran along my jawline.

A movement at the edge of the mirror made me jump; I was being watched. Lily stood in the doorway, her face wet with the tears that trickled silently down her face. I shed the coat and lifted her onto her parents' bed.

"What's wrong?" I asked.

Lily didn't say a word but continued to cry without a sound. I couldn't tell if she was tired or hungry or bored. Then I felt her bottom and jerked my hand back as if something had bit me.

I guessed that changing a baby couldn't be much worse than some of the things I had to do at the restaurant. Lily was no help, kicking and struggling so that when I was finished it looked like she was wearing a ball of paper, but at least she was dry. I thought how babies in China wore pants with the seat cut out, so that their bottoms stuck out like the halves of

wrinkled peaches, and they could relieve themselves whenever they wished. That seemed more practical.

Lily's clothes were wet, so I took her into her room and
changed her into her pajamas, but she didn't want to go to bed.
Remembering Jane's instructions, I found a book to read to her.
She refused to even sit on the bed, so we sat on the floor as I
read about rabbits who stole carrots from a garden and mice that
wrecked a dollhouse. Lily leaned against me and sucked her
thumb, and there was something comforting and familiar about
her warm, slightly damp presence. She didn't seem to mind when
I finished the book and started reading it again. Partway through
the third time her head lolled against my arm. I put her to bed
underneath sheets printed with pink tulips.

I returned to Jane and Richard's room to put everything
back the way I had found it. As I passed in front of the vanity
table, I caught my reflection in the mirror and stopped. Earlier, I had thought I looked like I was ready to go out to a
place with dim lighting and gentle music. Now the makeup
made my face look swollen, overripe, and I was reminded of
the painted courtesans on the snuff bottles over the fireplace.
While wiping my face clean in the bathroom, I noticed a row
of bottles behind the translucent shower curtain. One bottle
had a picture of a woman with hair the exact same color as
Jane's.

In the kitchen I checked the clock—it was almost nine—
and idly opened the refrigerator door to find cold green glass
bottles of water, jars of expensive-looking condiments, tubs
of beige spreads, and small pickled things. The cupboards revealed little more that looked familiar or edible. When I took
down a small flat tin to see what it was, the sound brought the
black cat purring around my ankles. One whole shelf was filled
with cans of diet cat food.

The kitchen window, which was lined with plants potted in white pebbles, looked out over a narrow air shaft into the apartment next door. While walking down streets in this neighborhood, I had often wondered what the interiors of the apartments looked like. But the sidewalk only gave me the view into someone's basement studio, or else a well-curtained front window. Now that I was on the same level, I could look all I wanted. I found that if I turned off the light, I could see clearly into the neighbors' kitchen, and it was better than television. I caught a glimpse of a woman's silk skirt, a flash of a man's white shirt collar. A wineglass and a bread knife. They were a young couple, I decided, newly married, with no children and impossibly happy. So happy that they didn't need to go out on a Saturday night and were staying in and cooking dinner instead.

The thought of their happiness made me feel all the more isolated. I dug my fingers into a plant on the windowsill until I could touch the roots. Then I selected the roundest pebble I could find and touched it briefly to my tongue. It tasted salty, like blood. I slipped it into my pocket. When I was a child and went to the seashore I would put a shell in my pocket. If I went to the mountains, it would be a leaf fallen from a tree. That way I would remember the places I had been, especially if I wasn't sure I would go back there.

When I looked up again, I couldn't believe what I saw. Outlined against the kitchen window across the air shaft were two naked bodies. Apparently the couple next door had gone from making dinner to making love. The light glazed their bare skin as they moved against the kitchen table, two people unconscious of anything outside of themselves. I could almost feel the edge of the table against the small of my own back. The plates and cups on the tabletop started to dance, until I was afraid they would fall and break. Then the couple moved to the floor where I couldn't see them anymore. I was just standing alone in a kitchen, in the dark, watching nothing.

I went back into the living room and switched the television to a news program. A policeman had been shot in Brooklyn and a deli owner had won eighty-five million dollars in the state lottery. In national news, more soldiers had died in Iraq. I sat in front of the television, looking not at the flashing movements on the screen but the brush painting on the wall.

It felt strange being in a real American home—although a lot of things in the apartment were not what I thought of as American, but Chinese. In addition to the snuff-bottle collection and the brush painting, I had noticed a hard green stone pillow being used as a doorstop in the bedroom, and a calligraphy scroll in the hallway. In a way it made sense, since Jane worked at a museum that specialized in Asian art. Then I remembered something Teacher Zhang had said once, that Americans had no culture so they were always trying to take on the culture of others. I wondered when Jane's interest in China had extended to adopting a baby.

I had been to an orphanage outside of Fuzhou once on a school field trip. Foreigners were not allowed to visit, we were told, because they would spread lies about the orphans' living conditions and make the Chinese government look bad. We'd taken a short-distance bus there—the thirty-five girls in my class, a few peasants returning from their morning trip to the market, and our home economics teacher, Teacher Miao.

Teacher Miao was a spinsterish woman in her forties who was supposed to teach us the practical things in life, like what jobs we might get in the future, if we were lucky. For example, the week before, we had gone on a field trip to a state-run factory that produced bread. Our mouths watered from the scent of freshly baked rolls, but Teacher Miao told us we couldn't sample anything because it belonged to the collective.

As my classmates chattered and laughed and teased each other about the pictures of pop stars adorning their notebooks, I stared out the window of the bus. Fields passed in a green wave. Oxen waded knee-deep in mud, followed by men burned brown from the sun. The few houses that could be seen from the road were built in the traditional style, with the tips of the roof pointed toward the sky like the upward strokes of an ink brush. I thought about what it must be like to live in one of those houses. Although I had grown up in town, many of my classmates were from local villages and could go home only during the holidays. After spring festival they'd return with packets of sticky rice cakes and jars of pickled vegetables, and that night the dorm room would be filled with the sound of muffled weeping. I didn't know then what it felt like to be away from home.

When we arrived at the orphanage, which was a concrete-and-tile building much like our school, we were met by a smiling representative who explained to us how the place worked. Many of the children had been found in markets or by the sides of the roads, with little more than the blankets they were wrapped in. They had been given the last name of Jiang, after the president of China at the time. Very few were adopted, other than by peasant families who needed another hand to help with the farming or to take care of elderly relatives. When they got older, some went to town to make a living; others were hired to work at the orphanage itself.

Swallow, who was standing next to me, squeezed my arm. "What a sad life!" she whispered.

I nodded, but then the orphanage's representative said we would be allowed to take a look at the babies, and everyone squealed with delight. To us, babies were as enigmatic as boys. Most of us had no experience with babies, as we didn't have younger brothers or sisters. One classmate had a little "cousin" who visited from the countryside, but we all knew this was actually a little sister who had been spirited away to be raised by relatives.

We were led into a room where the babies lay in communal cribs. Their faces were scrunched against the light and their fists banged against the air. A child minder sat in the corner but she made no effort to pick up any of the babies who were crying. My classmates looked around at each other; this was not what we had expected.

"Look carefully, girls," Teacher Miao said. "If you're not careful, this could be in your future."

I glanced at Teacher Miao's face. There appeared to be a smile in the corner of her mouth, as if she enjoyed scaring us. No wonder she never married, I thought to myself.

~ ~ ~

I awoke to the faded fragrance from Jane's wrist as she shook me awake. She said, "You fell asleep on the couch."

As my mind cleared I could hear a thin wail from down the hall. "Oh, no." I scrambled to my feet.

"It's okay. Richard's gone to check on her."

I looked at the clock on the DVD player and saw that it was almost twelve. "We're later than we thought," Jane said. "Did everything go all right here?"

I nodded, wondering if I had remembered to leave the bathroom light on for Lily. But I knew that was nothing compared to my falling asleep on the job, even if I had been exhausted from standing all day at work.

Richard came into the living room holding Lily. Her face was red and blotchy, but she was quiet. "I think we woke her up coming in," he said. "She hadn't been crying long."

"I'm sorry," I said. "I didn't mean—"

"It's fine," Jane interrupted. "No one's hurt or anything." She didn't sound angry, but I caught the look she exchanged with Richard. "It's late and we won't keep you any longer."

I said good night to Richard and to Lily, who turned away from me and buried her face in her father's neck. Jane accompanied me to the door. She gave me two bills, then pressed a third into my hand. "This is for a taxi home," she said. "Be safe."

I thanked her and left. Once I stepped out of the building, I felt the warmth of the summer night wash over me, along with relief that I had gotten through the evening. I looked at the bills Jane had given me. With the extra for the taxi, it was more than I'd make on the busiest day at the restaurant, even with tips. I folded the bills and put them in my pocket, my fingers lingering on the white pebble I'd taken from the kitchen. Then I headed toward the nearest subway.

Chapter Six

As the summer went on, I had to embellish the story about my sick aunt to get out of work so I could continue to babysit Lily. Now my aunt wasn't merely sick, she had pneumonia, and I had to stay with her once a week to give my poor uncle a rest. By this time the other restaurant workers had heard about this, and they also knew I was hiding something. Xiao Ru thought I was seeing a boy, while Gao was convinced I was winning big money at a secret mah-jongg game. Old Chou grumbled at first, but his relative who was there for the summer continued to fill in for me, and I gave up taking my one afternoon off during the week.

Because I could no longer go to the park during the day, Saturday night was the only time I could see Lily. This was not every week; sometimes the Templeton-Walkers spent the weekend at their house in the country. Although by now I knew that only certain New Yorkers could afford to keep a country home, I couldn't help picturing Jane and Richard and

Lily in a mud-brick cottage like peasants, with a shared out-house down the road and chickens coming in through the front door. Most Saturdays, however, they were in the city, and now it was my name that Lily called when the doorbell rang.

When I arrived, Jane would be rushing through the apart-ment in a fancy new dress—I never saw her wear the same thing twice—as she prepared to go out. She'd apply a last touch of makeup, grab her purse, and kiss Lily before she left. But her presence was strong and comforting when she was gone. It was in the scent of her perfume, in the way the flowers on the table were arranged, the shape of her handwriting on the notes she left for me on the refrigerator.

I saw more of Richard than Jane, as he waited for her to get ready. Before, I had been oblivious to his role in Jane's and Lily's life, but now I saw how Lily's face brightened when he came home and how easily she ran to him. I noticed how when he and Jane left the apartment his hand rested at her elbow in guidance as much as protection. Still, I thought of him as sepa-rate from his wife and daughter. In the rare moments that I saw the three of them together, Richard seemed to hover at the edges of the room, as if he had come in late to the party.

I thought of my job less like babysitting and more like try-ing to find the magic key that would make Lily fall asleep at the end of an evening. It was never the same thing two weeks in a row. Sometimes it was the DVD with the oddly colored animals, other times it was a picture book that she had me read so many times I started jumbling the words until she corrected me. Finally she'd fall asleep and I'd put her into bed, tucking the blanket firmly around her and remembering to leave the bathroom light on.

After Lily went to sleep, the apartment was all mine. I'd go through the kitchen, brave enough now to sample the strange contents of the refrigerator. I'd pick up the photos scattered throughout the rooms, their silver or gilt frames heavy in my hands: a picture of baby Lily, her hair sticking straight up; a snapshot of an older Lily, hair now tamed, sitting in Jane's lap; a black-and-white wedding photo of Jane and Richard. There was a peculiar contradiction of time in that last photo with the sepia tint that made it look deliberately old, the classic cuts of Jane's dress and Richard's suit, the fact that Jane and Richard themselves looked hardly younger than they presently were. Maybe Jane was a bit thinner then and Richard had more hair, but they looked timeless. Later I realized this just meant that Jane and Richard had not been married for as long as I'd thought.

In Jane's desk I found a schedule book of fine red leather. Through her clear, precise script, amid various jottings of dinners and playdates and doctors' appointments, I discovered that she went to see a Dr. Silver on Park Avenue every Tuesday. The only other constant entry was "lunch with Evan," but when I flipped back through the pages, Jane had apparently stopped having "lunch with Evan" when the summer started. Lying on Jane and Richard's bed, the schedule book open before me, I imagined that Jane had been having an affair with Evan, a young, clean-shaven banker type who wore blue suits instead of brown. She would meet him while she was out in the park with Lily, until Richard spied on them one day. I laughed to myself when I imagined Richard hiding behind a tree, looking like a bear in his brown suit.

~ ~ ~

In the beginning of July, I received a call from my aunt, the one who was supposedly sick. I had not heard from Uncle

George or Aunt May since the day I had moved into the boardinghouse in Chinatown. After they had picked me up at the airport I'd spent a couple of days with them at their home in New Jersey. Uncle George had taken me into Chinatown, to an employment agency for new immigrants. By the next morning the agency had found me a waitressing job and, through my new employer, a place to live. Before I left, Aunt May had pressed her youngest daughter's old coat on me and said that she and my uncle would have me over to visit soon. But until that summer day, neither of them had contacted me.

Now Aunt May wanted to know if I'd like to spend the coming weekend in New Jersey with them. There was going to be a fireworks display at the local high school, and they thought I might want to celebrate with them, seeing as it was my first Fourth of July in America. I replied that the restaurant did not let us take off any holidays, which was true. We worked on Thanksgiving and Christmas and the lunar New Year—Old Chou didn't care whether the holiday was American or Chinese. But Aunt May persisted, so I agreed to ask for Saturday afternoon to Sunday afternoon off. My concern wasn't about missing work at the restaurant, but that I would have to cancel babysitting Lily that Saturday night.

When I called Jane to tell her this, my voice was faint. I was afraid that she would think I was trying to get out of work but she sounded like it was the most natural thing in the world that I would want to do.

"Of course you should spend time with your aunt and uncle," she said. "I didn't know you had relatives here. Where do they live?"

"New Jersey."

"That's nice. They must have a large house and backyard." She sounded almost envious.

"Yes, they do." It felt like their house was in the middle of the woods, with enormous tree branches arching over the roof and shading the lawn. "I am sorry to call so late. Can you find someone to babysit Lily?"

"Oh, don't worry about it. Richard and I might stay home, or at least I might stay home—that would be a good excuse not to go out, wouldn't it? We've been too dependent on you, expecting you to come over and babysit for us anytime. Of course you're going to have other things to do on a Saturday night."

Besides work at the restaurant there wasn't anything else in my life, but I knew that wasn't what Jane wanted to hear. She saw me in a certain way, as if I were no different than the other young people she knew, or how she had once been.

So, early that Saturday afternoon, I took public transportation to New Jersey. When the bus emerged from the tunnel leading out of Manhattan, I looked back to see the tall buildings wavering in the heat. I couldn't imagine what it had looked like with the Twin Towers; they had fallen before I had come to New York, and I knew them only through postcards sold on the street.

The New Jersey town that my aunt and uncle lived in consisted of houses separated by wide lawns. The single main street was lined with stores and a gas station at either end; the largest buildings were the library, high school, and community center. Aunt May and Uncle George were waiting at the bus stop to pick me up in their car, although if I remembered correctly, the bus stop was only a few blocks from where they lived.

"How nice to see you, Hua," Aunt May said, giving me a hug that smelled like cut grass. "We think of you every time we go into Chinatown."

Uncle George shook my hand; he smelled of mothballs. "How is your grandmother?" he asked.

"She was well in her last letter. Don't you hear from her?"

"Oh, sometimes," Aunt May replied.

We got into the car and put on our seat belts for the short ride. For my benefit, Uncle George had us circle the high school where the town's residents watched the fireworks every year from the football field.

"They shoot them off from the river," Uncle George said.

"How would you know?" Aunt May said, and added to me, "Just because he studied engineering in Taiwan. The river's too far away for that."

I half listened to them argue with each other as to where the fireworks display could be coming from, something they apparently had not discussed in all the years they had watched it. My grandmother had told me that Uncle George met Aunt May, who was American-born, at a dance in Chinatown. This must have been in the sixties, when in America women wore flip hairdos and men sported wide-legged trousers, and back in China people were busy persecuting each other.

My grandmother's story continued: Uncle George met Aunt May at a dance, they got married and had two girls, and moved from the city to New Jersey. Uncle George had been a mechanic and Aunt May had been a real estate agent, but now they were both retired. During my first visit, Aunt May had spent most of her time outside gardening while Uncle George sat in the den and bought items sold on television. They seemed to enter the circle of each other's existence only for meals, although they told me they took many vacations together—visits to California where their daughters lived, as well as cruises to the Caribbean and trips to Europe. As proof, their house was crammed with souvenirs. There were dish towels embroidered with Dutch windmills, a stained-glass reproduction of the *Mona Lisa* hanging in the window, a mini Leaning Tower of Pisa in the china cabinet.

After lunch, I helped Aunt May in the garden with her rosebushes. Last fall they had been covered with burlap, looking like old women hunched over in the cold, but now they bloomed dark red and white and yellow-flecked pink. As she described the special mulch she used, I noticed Aunt May looking my way several times as if she wished she could use her pruning shears on me.

"I pulled out some more of the girls' old clothes from the attic," she finally said. "They should fit you."

I thought of the worn black coat she had made me take last time, and then all the pretty clothes in Jane's closet. "No, thank you," I said. "It is too much trouble for you."

"*Mei guanxi,*" she said. "It's nothing. I was going to throw them out anyway. It's too warm where the girls live now, they don't need stuff like that. But you do, and things are expensive in New York. I would take them if I were you." I knew she was hinting that I was in no position to refuse.

"I think I'll go inside now," I said.

"It's too hot out here," Aunt May agreed. "You should go and visit with your uncle. He's had nothing to do since he retired."

As I had suspected, Uncle George was sitting in the den where it was relatively cool, facing the television. When I came in, he lowered the sound a notch.

"How is your job?" he asked.

I thought of telling him about babysitting for the Templeton-Walkers but that would be too hard to explain. "It's not bad, although the hours are long."

"What else do you expect?"

I shrugged. "I didn't expect to work at a restaurant, I guess."

Uncle George stared at me over his cup of tea, and I looked away. Last year, when I had first arrived in this country, I would have been willing to do just about anything for a job, and I wouldn't have dared behave this way toward my sponsors. Then Uncle George lifted the stained lid of his cup and took a meditative sip.

"I know your grandmother said you were a smart girl, but there are many people who come to this country with degrees and have to take any job they can get. How do you think I got started?"

I wondered if I had offended him. My grandmother told me that Uncle George had come to the States with papers saying he was the son of a man who owned a restaurant. He'd had to work at that place for years to pay off his debts.

"I started out as dishwasher number two. After a year I became dishwasher number one. Then in a year I became a cook. Guess what happened next."

"You became the manager?"

"No! I attended night school and only went back to the restaurant as a customer!" Uncle George laughed, spluttering his tea. "You have to learn to be humble in this country first, no matter how long it takes. Then you can have all this."

I looked around the room, which also seemed to be the repository for all the things Uncle George bought through the television. There were unopened boxes with exercise equipment, mixing machines, knife sets, and air purifiers. But I knew that he meant the house and the furniture in it, the backyard, the vacations, even the two daughters who lived on the other side of the country. That was the accumulation of his life.

Just before sunset, Uncle George, Aunt May, and I got into the car and drove back to the high school. By now there were people sitting on blankets spread across the ground and eating the last of their picnic dinners. Everyone's faces were turned expectantly to the east, confirming Uncle George's theory that the fireworks were shot off from the river. Aunt May had brought an old flowered sheet for us to sit on, and in the settling dusk we looked like all the other families.

Occasional glints of light pricked the dark fabric of the crowd—fireflies and sparklers carried by children with too much energy. When the fireworks began, I thought the bursts of light and sound would scare the children. But murmurs of amazement rose around me as dense as the smoke that soon began drifting across the sky. I was reminded of the children back home who would run down the street ahead of the lion dancers at the lunar New Year, firecrackers popping at their heels.

Uncle George gripped my shoulder to get my attention. "They might be celebrating the freedom of America," he said, "but remember, fireworks were invented in China!"

It wasn't that late when we got home, but Aunt May went to bed and Uncle George turned on the television to watch the end of the fireworks being set off in Washington, D.C. Earlier he had told me that in recent years he and Aunt May hadn't bothered to go out to the football field and just watched the fireworks on television, but this year was special because I was there. Restless, I wandered into the backyard, which was dark except for a glow behind the treetops where I imagined New York lay. Compared to the city, even with the hum of crickets, this place was eerily quiet.

I could see why Jane sounded envious on the phone when she had mentioned a house and a backyard. If she and Richard lived in a place like this, there would be many rooms for Lily to run through and a swing set she could play on. In my mind, I began replacing things from my aunt and uncle's home with things from Jane and Richard's apartment: jars of olives instead of Chinese vegetables, fine art in the place of kitschy souvenirs, stacks of books replacing unopened boxes of household gadgets. I continued, imagining Jane tending roses in the garden while Richard holed up in the den. And Lily would run across the lawn in crazy circles, streams of light flowing from the sparklers clasped in her hands.

I stopped in the den to say good night to Uncle George, but he had fallen asleep in his recliner. I turned off the television and went upstairs. The room I was staying in used to belong to my aunt and uncle's younger daughter, the one whose coat I now owned. It looked barely touched, as if a little girl still lived there. The furniture was butter yellow to match the wallpaper and a ruffled canopy arched over the twin bed. The bookcase held an encyclopedia set and novels about sturdy female pioneers. On the walls, school photos of a girl with braces progressed to one of an older girl in a fancy dress, the arm of a boy who was not Chinese around her shoulders.

I looked closely at these pictures but I couldn't see any physical resemblance between this girl and me. Yet I could imagine Lily growing up to look like her: a girl with the kind of brash smile that came from living in America. I looked through the desk drawers and found old test papers proclaiming As and Bs in English and geometry. In the back of one drawer was a book with a flowered cloth cover whose lock popped open with a single tug. A round, childish script stared back at me, the *is* dotted with tiny hearts. I didn't read far before I came across the statement *I hate my parents.* I wondered how anyone could hate the same people who had given them food and clothes, a place to live, and the chance for an education. But whether that thought was right or wrong, I had to envy this girl for being so secure of her parents' love that she could dare to hate them.

When I went to sleep I dreamed that I was looking from the bedroom window onto the dark lawn. All I could see was Lily running away from me toward the far corner of the backyard, her tiny white dress like a moth in the night.

~   ~   ~

The next morning Uncle George offered to drive me into the city, but I said I would be fine taking the bus. I left with a shopping bag of old clothes that Aunt May had convinced me to take. She also gave me a tin of butter cookies, a package of salted plums, and a plastic container of dried shredded pork. I figured that these things had been bought at some point in Chinatown, and now they were going back there.

The following Saturday evening Jane asked me how my visit with my relatives had gone. I made a few remarks about how much fun I had had, and how I wished I could see them more often, but the truth was I did not think I would be going back to New Jersey anytime soon. The sense I'd got from my aunt and uncle when I'd left was that their obligation was done as far as I was concerned.

"You're lucky," Jane said. "My family's back in Minnesota, and Richard's relatives—the ones that he speaks to, that is— are scattered along the East Coast. It would be nice for Lily to grow up knowing her aunts and uncles and cousins. I can't help feeling that back in China, she'd be part of one huge extended family, and we're cheating her out of that experience somehow."

I didn't tell her that not everyone had that kind of family.

A few weeks later, Jane asked me to come a little earlier to their apartment. When I arrived Richard had come home from work, and both he and Jane looked ready to go out. I followed Jane into the kitchen and sat at the counter as I had the first time I'd been there; Jane faced me from the other side, the palms of her hands flat against the surface.

"It's like this," she said. "We really, really like having you come over to babysit Lily. She likes you a lot, she talks about you all the time when you're not here. 'Hua read me this book,' she says, 'Hua told me this story.'"

My heart sank at the tone of Jane's voice. She sounded like she was stalling, trying to figure out how to tell me that she no longer needed me to babysit without upsetting me. I nodded, as if that would make it easier for the both of us.

"So Richard and I were thinking that maybe you'd be able to babysit her on the afternoons during the week. As your job."

I was still nodding. I blurted out the first thing in my head. "What about Margarita?"

Jane looked surprised. "She went back to Ecuador in June—that's where she's from. Her family is there."

A picture of Margarita flashed into my mind: a young woman with long, curly dark hair in a dense green jungle, being welcomed home by her parents, maybe even a child of her own.

"She mostly came on the weekends, maybe a couple of afternoons a week. She also took care of another child, so we couldn't always get her to sit. Anyway, your situation would be different. We'd still need you to come the occasional Saturday night, but we—well, I—would really need you on weekday afternoons. You see, I'm going to go back to work part-time at the museum in the fall."

"I already have a job," I said, but I wasn't sure if I was speaking to Jane or myself. I thought about the stifling heat from the kitchen at the restaurant, the sticky residue of grease, the constant noise of clattering dishes.

"I know, we'll have to talk about payment. But you won't have to do any housekeeping or anything like that. I'd leave for work after lunch, and I'd be back in time to give Lily her dinner and her bath. Really, you wouldn't have to do much more than what you're doing here already. Except, well . . . I was hoping that maybe you'd speak some Chinese with Lily, teach her a little bit about her culture."

"Will it be useful for her here?"

"Of course! Even if she weren't Chinese, the language is all the rage around here. Kids are learning it in preschool, and seriously, Mandarin-speaking nannies are a hot commodity on the Upper West Side."

"But why?"

Jane shrugged. "People think the future is in China."

I still didn't believe her, but the idea of myself as Lily's caretaker was starting to take shape in my mind. One thought bothered me, though: Jane wanted me to be a role model for Lily, to teach her how to be Chinese. I didn't know if I could do it.

"I thought you could start a week before I go back to work, so I could be around in case you had any questions. If this is what you want, of course." Since I still hadn't said anything, Jane added, "Well, why don't you think it over. Talk to your boss, see if it's worth your while."

"I would like to," I said. "Except—"

Jane leaned over the counter. "Yes?"

"Are you asking me only because I am from China?"

She laughed. "Yes, partly. If possible, I'd want the person who takes care of Lily to be somebody from the country of her ancestors. But also, I'm asking you because you're like me."

I stared at her, at her red hair and green eyes. "How?"

"You remind me of me when I first came to New York."

When we went back into the living room, I was surprised to see Lily and Richard there as if nothing had happened, as if our lives weren't all going to be different from now on. Jane excused herself to finish getting ready, and I sat down on the floor next to Lily. She was busy jumping on a pile of books, smashing the bindings one way and the other. I wouldn't let a child do that to my books, but Richard made no move to do anything about it, and I figured it was his house.

After a minute or so of Lily's gleeful jumping, Richard turned to me and said, sounding almost desperate, "Hua, can you make her stop doing that?"

"Lily," I said. "Stop."

To my surprise—and, I suspect, Richard's—she did. It was then that I understood why he had asked me to discipline her. From now on, Lily was my responsibility.

Part III

Chapter Seven

Dear Hua,

Pei and I have moved into our own house. It is not far from the stop for the bus that we take to work, and it is in a quiet neighborhood. We can also take a bus to a part of town that has Chinese supermarkets and restaurants. It's not like Chinatown, though, it is cleaner and more spread apart. Also, most of the people are from Taiwan and have money, and they act like it, too. Still, it is good to be in a place where you can get mooncakes for Mid-Autumn Festival. Now that I have an address, please write to me to tell me how you are doing. Also, if you can get time off from Old Chou (ha) maybe you can come and visit?

Your friend,
Ah Jing

I checked the top left-hand corner of the envelope in which Ah Jing's letter had arrived. The street she lived on was called

Ocean Boulevard, in Los Angeles. I pictured a row of houses alongside a beach, the surf crashing in the distance. Ah Jing's house was the one with the orange trees in the front yard and the pink tiled roof.

I had not heard from Ah Jing for months, not even a postcard. All that time I had wanted to write her, to tell her about meeting Jane and Lily in the park, the Saturday nights spent babysitting, my new job as Lily's nanny. But now that she had an address I could write to, my hand was heavy with reluctance. I was afraid that by writing these things down, I was guaranteeing they would go sour.

I could have written Ah Jing about how Old Chou had called me ungrateful and slammed a door in my face when I had quit my job at the restaurant. I could have told her about the week that I spent with Jane and Lily, before Jane went back to work. I had gone with them to the grocery store where Jane purchased the strange items that went into her refrigerator, to children's toy and clothing stores, to story hour at the library, and to the park.

Each afternoon before we left the house, Jane would tell me what to put in the diaper bag that she hung from the stroller. In addition to diapers and a changing pad, there was mineral water, juice boxes, snacks packed individually in plastic bags, pacifiers, Band-Aids, changes of clothing, sweaters, umbrellas, storybooks, and a favorite doll or stuffed animal. It always seemed like we were about to embark on a long trip. Preparing to go out also took a long time because Jane would change Lily into a dress or do her hair.

Once, after she had fixed Lily's bangs back with a barrette made of rhinestones, she stood her daughter in front of a mirror.

"Doesn't your hair look pretty now?" Jane said. "Aren't you the most beautiful little girl in the world?"

Lily gazed at her reflection in the mirror and nodded so that her sparkling forelock bounced up and down.

Jane looked at me as if for support.

"Yes," I agreed. "You are most beautiful."

Lily clapped her hands and laughed.

"I read somewhere that it's important to reassure adopted children from Asia that they're attractive," Jane said, "since they don't have as many role models on television or in magazines as other minorities do."

"Aren't you afraid that she will grow up"—I searched for the word—"vain?"

Jane shrugged. "It's better that she has a good opinion of herself than a bad one, especially when it comes to her appearance. When I was growing up, my mother constantly told me I should lose weight. I want Lily to think she is beautiful, no matter what she looks like."

That, I supposed, was worth something. The best compliment I could have received as a child was that I was quiet or obedient. Certainly my grandmother had never told me I was pretty. It had probably never occurred to her that I might have wanted to hear it. I would look at the pictures of my mother as a young woman before she was sent away for re-education. In one she is wearing a *qipao* that is cut out of plain, coarse cloth. But she looks as proud as if it were her wedding dress.

~ ~ ~

On my first afternoon alone as Lily's nanny, I broke one of Jane's rules.

Outside of the house, I was allowed to take Lily to the park and nowhere else. Jane did not want me running errands for her, or, she implied, for myself. This might change later, she said, but for now she thought it would be best if we stuck to the house and the park.

But at noon, just before leaving the boardinghouse, I had received a message from Old Chou, via Mrs. Chou and Mrs. Ma, that I should come to the restaurant immediately to pick up my last paycheck. Since I had not left the restaurant on good terms, I'd decided I would forgo my paycheck so I wouldn't have to run into Old Chou again. Obviously he felt the same way; the message was that if I wanted to get my check, I had to pick it up by five o'clock that same day while he was out.

That afternoon, Lily looked at me questioningly when we turned down a different street from the one we usually took to the park.

"Where we going?" she asked.

"We're going on an adventure," I told her. "It'll be fun, you'll see." I sounded much more confident than I felt. If Jane found out that I had disobeyed her on my first day alone on the job, she might fire me.

I descended the stairs into the sticky throat of the subway station, the stroller against one hip and Lily on the other. I supposed most mothers in the city could afford to take cabs. In the train car Lily climbed up on one of the seats to look out the window. The flashing lights in the subway tunnel were reflected in her eyes like distant stars.

The car was almost empty at that time of day. An unshaven man with bare feet lay sprawled across several seats, snoring. Two dark-complexioned men sitting opposite each other conversed in a foreign language, their words arcing back and forth in the air like balls they would never drop. An elderly woman sitting near us looked up from her book at Lily and me and smiled. I smiled back, realizing what she thought she saw: a woman and her daughter on an outing together.

When we were above ground again, I made Lily get into the stroller even though she wanted to walk. I was afraid I might lose her in the grime and noise of Canal Street. As we moved slowly eastward, Lily stared at the various items spilling from the storefronts: buckets of colorful plastic toys, slippers made out of cheap brocade, delicate paper fans that said "I ♥ New York." I wondered how often Jane and Richard took her to Chinatown.

The moment we stopped, Lily's hand shot out and grabbed a toy dog whose semidetached head could nod and shake from side to side, as if it were very confused.

"Want this," she announced.

"Lily, put that back," I said. I tried to take it from her but she held on with unexpected force.

"Want!" I could hear the whirlwind of a tantrum rising in that one word.

The shopkeeper came out to see what was going on.

"How much?" I asked him in Mandarin.

"Five dollars."

"That's too much," I replied.

"Four dollars, then."

"For this flimsy thing?"

"Okay, three-fifty."

"Forget it." I pried the toy from Lily's fingers and put it back, then made as if to leave.

"Three dollars!" the shopkeeper called after me.

I turned around. As I handed the toy to Lily, I whispered to her, "That's how you bargain."

She looked up at me and nodded, clutching her toy.

I entered through the back door of the Lucky Duck to see a scene familiar from slow afternoons. Li and Gao were smoking and playing cards, slapping them down as if the louder the sound, the more clever the move. Xiao Ru was on the phone dealing with an irate customer.

"Yes, sir. . . . No, sir. . . ." she said, then stopped speaking altogether. When she saw me, she waved frantically.

"I don't know what to do," she told me. "I can't understand him. When I ask him to slow down, he just speaks louder."

I took the receiver from her but had to hold it a few inches away from my ear.

"What is wrong with you people? Why don't any of you bother to learn English? You've bothered to open a restaurant in this country, but you can't even speak the goddamn language? If I moved to another country you bet your goddamn ass I'd . . ."

Xiao Ru's eyes met mine over the telephone.

"It's hopeless," I said and let the receiver dangle from its cord. We watched it as though it were a dying animal, until the sputtering faded away.

"What are you doing back here?" Gao asked me. "And who's this little doll?" He indicated Lily.

"She's mine," I boasted.

"What?" Xiao Ru stared at me. "I didn't know you had a child."

"She's kidding," Gao said. "That's not hers."

"What do you mean?" I said. "I mean, you're right, but how did you know?"

Gao shrugged. "Her clothes are too nice. Me, when I was that age, wore just underpants. My parents were too poor to afford anything else."

"We wore nothing," Li contributed. "What? It was too hot for clothes."

"Is she why you left the restaurant?" Xiao Ru asked.

"I take care of her for a rich American couple," I said. "She's adopted."

There were uniform clucks of sympathy from everyone.

"It's a pity," Xiao Ru said.

"Yes," Li added. "She'll grow up knowing nothing about her homeland. She'll be worse than those American-born Chinese."

"Can she even talk?" Gao asked. "She looks kind of stupid."

Xiao Ru hit him on the arm. "She can't understand Chinese."

I lifted Lily from the stroller and set her on the counter. "Say your name," I instructed her in English. She looked at me, squirming a little. "Come on, tell them."

"I knew she was stupid," Gao muttered.

"Lily Templon-Walker," Lily's clear, childish voice rang out.

"Templeton-Walker," I corrected.

"What kind of name is that?"

"That's a long name for such a little girl."

"How old are you, Lily?" I said, ignoring the comments.

"Two and a half."

Everyone seemed impressed by that. I alone knew that according to Lily, she had been "two and a half" for months now, and she was really almost three.

"See?" I said. "She's smart."

"Huh." Gao snorted. "A parrot can be trained to say anything."

Xiao Ru noticed the toy dog in the stroller and brought it over to Lily, shaking it so that the head waggled back and forth. "Is this your little dog?" she said in Chinese. "Here's your little dog. . . ."

"Did Old Chou say anything to you about my paycheck?" I asked Gao.

"Actually, he did. Come with me."

I asked Xiao Ru to watch Lily and followed Gao into the storeroom. He closed the door behind us, then took the cash box down from a shelf and fumbled with the keys at his waist.

"Here." He tossed an envelope at me.

I checked the bills inside. Old Chou had been generous. I pictured his lined face, weary and disappointed as I had last seen it, and regretted the manner in which I had left. But he would find someone to replace me soon enough.

When I turned around, I saw Gao standing between me and the closed door. He made no sign of moving. The expression on his face was serious. "I have something important to offer you."

"What?" I said, trying to ignore the garlic on his breath.

"Well . . . I was thinking . . . now that you're not working here anymore. . . . I was thinking that you and I . . ." He looked flushed, though maybe it was because of the lack of air in the storeroom. "Xiao Ru is better looking than you, but . . . you know . . . she's not that bright. And you . . . you know a lot of English already. We could open our own restaurant, if we were . . . you know . . ."

For a moment I stared at him, the thought too ridiculous to consider. "What, so you can boss me around and I can pick up your cigarette butts?" I started to laugh and Gao got redder.

"Forget it," he muttered. "You're no different than any other fresh-off-the-boat girl. You want a *laowai* to come save you, to take you away from all this. Some American guy with money so you can get your green card."

My spine snapped straight. "Who are you calling a *laowai*?" I shouted. "Take a look around you. You're the foreigner here! Even if you have your own restaurant, you'll never leave Chinatown."

Gao crossed his arms, grinning. "Well, at least I know where I belong."

I ducked under his arm and opened the storeroom door. I said good-bye to Xiao Ru and Li, bundled Lily into the stroller, and left. I vowed that I would never go back to the Lucky Duck, not even as a customer.

~ ~ ~

On the way back, I realized I had to make sure Lily didn't tell Jane where we had gone. Lily talked quite a lot now, maybe not in complete sentences, but enough to give me away. I stopped the stroller on the sidewalk and bent down so my face was level with hers.

"Lily, if Mommy asks where we go today, you say, 'the park.' Okay?"

"The park," Lily repeated.

"Lily," I said, imitating Jane's voice. "Where did you go today?"

Lily turned so she was looking back in the direction we had come. "Takeout?"

"No!" That would be a disaster. "How about, 'for a walk'?"

"A walk." Lily looked up at me hopefully, her eyes large and dark. It was a look I was starting to recognize as indicating she wanted someone's approval, and it was impossible to refuse her.

I kissed the top of her head. "Perfect."

When we got back to the apartment it was past three and time for Lily's nap. She woke up by the time Jane came home.

"Hello, baby," Jane said, hugging Lily to her. "I missed you so much today. Did you and Hua have a good time?"

Lily nodded, still slow and small-eyed from sleep.

"What did you do today?"

I bit my lip, willing Lily to say something blameless.

She looked at me and said, "Takeout?"

I held my breath.

"Sure, honey, we can get takeout," Jane said. "We'll decide before Daddy gets home and surprise him." She started toward the kitchen with Lily in her arms, then stopped as if the thought had just occurred to her. "Hua, would you like to stay for dinner?"

I gulped and nodded, just glad that I hadn't been found out.

In the kitchen, Jane produced a sheaf of take-out menus from a drawer and let Lily choose. Although there were menus from Chinese, Indian, Thai, and Vietnamese restaurants, Lily immediately pointed toward the menu from the sushi place. I guessed it was the most appealing to a child with its colored pictures, but I couldn't help shaking my head over this little Chinese girl who preferred sushi over Chinese food.

Jane was in her room when the buzzer rang.

"Hua, can you get that?" she called. "I'm in the middle of changing. The money's on the counter. Just press the button by the door."

I opened the door to the expressionless face of a delivery boy who, oddly enough, looked more Chinese than Japanese. Lily clutched my legs and looked out from behind me, both bold and safe at the same time. I looked at the receipt, then at the bills Jane had left. She had ordered a large amount and it was quite expensive. Still, she had provided more than enough money, so I added an extra-big tip.

"Thank you very much," the delivery boy said, bobbing his head. He said it like it was one word—*thankyouverymuch*—the way Xiao Ru did at the end of taking orders on the phone. It had always irked me because it sounded so submissive and wrong. The delivery boy must have thought that I lived in this apartment. I nodded graciously to keep up the illusion and closed the door before he had turned to leave.

By the time Richard came home, Jane and I had transferred the circlets of rice and fish and seaweed and pink petals of ginger onto dinner plates so that they looked like small flower arrangements. Although I knew what sushi was, I had never eaten it, so I picked out the most harmless-looking items— the chunk of bean curd that was unexpectedly filled with rice, the slices of cooked eel. At Jane's urging I took a piece of raw pink fish and forced myself to swallow it. It felt like someone else's tongue in my mouth.

Richard tried to teach Lily the names of the different kinds of sushi. "That's *otoro,*" he said, putting a piece of fish onto her plate. "That's *hamachi.*"

Lily piled the pieces of sushi on top of each other like blocks, took a nibble of vinegared rice from one, then knocked the stack down.

"Don't play with your food, Lily," Jane said, but Lily was pushing her food around on her plate as if it were a toy train. "She's such a picky eater these days," Jane commented and neatly flipped one of the uneaten pieces onto her own plate, then into her mouth, with her chopsticks.

I was secretly amazed at how well both Jane and Richard used their chopsticks. Although some Americans who came to the Lucky Duck were expert users, there were also those who asked for forks, or dropped things on the floor or the tablecloth, requiring extra cleaning later. Lily just used her fingers. I tried to recall if I had learned how to use chopsticks at her age. All I could remember was my grandmother feeding me from her own bowl, picking out the fattiest cubes of pork or freshest bits of greens to put in my mouth.

Jane and Richard started talking about what they had done that day as if I weren't there. Bits of their conversation faded in and out of my attention.

". . . she's awful, acting like I might as well not bother to come in at all if I'm only there part time. . . ."

". . . what's awful is this new playwright everyone's talking about, like he's the second Edward Albee or something. . . ."

". . . as if she remembers what it's like to have a child under five, bet she was on antidepressants the whole time. . . ."

". . . it's like something I would have written back in the eighties, and you know how bad that was. . . ."

I glanced up in the middle of a sudden silence to see Jane and Richard looking at each other across the table, unformed words hovering in the space between them.

Then Richard said, softly, "Maybe you shouldn't have gone back there."

"Then where do you suggest I should have gone?"

"Any number of galleries would have taken you. You're qualified enough."

"I'm well aware of that. There just aren't that many galleries that deal specifically with Asian art. *Contemporary* Asian art." Jane's hand shot up like a knife blade. "And don't suggest teaching again."

"I wasn't about to."

Jane turned her attention to Lily. "I told you not to play with your food!" She swept up the mess on Lily's plate in one quick, exasperated gesture and began piling up the empty plastic take-out containers. I moved to help her, but she said, "No, Hua, please don't do that."

I sat back in my chair, helpless, as Jane continued to collect the unused soy sauce packets and disposable chopsticks. Richard seemed not to know what to do either. Then he picked Lily up and said as if to no one, "I'll get her ready for her bath," and left the room noiselessly. For a man his size I was constantly surprised by how quiet he was when he entered or left a room.

I watched as Jane put the plates in the dishwasher and continued to run the sponge over the tabletop long after the surface was clean.

"I'm sorry you had to see that," she said.

I almost jumped. I didn't think she had remembered I was still in the room.

"It's been a long day. First day back at work in almost two years. People look at you differently. I was on maternity leave for some of that time, but . . . I just think they would be more understanding if it were for a natural child, you know?" She murmured as if to herself, "Of course you don't know."

"I know," I heard myself saying.

Jane looked at me for a long moment, as if she couldn't understand why I had said that. I didn't know, myself. There was no way I could have known what Jane was thinking or feeling, no matter how many times I put on her makeup, or tried on her clothes, or looked through her private things. But I had known, in that moment of fleeting clarity, what she had wanted to hear.

"Well," Jane said, wiping her hands on a dish towel, "shall we go see how Richard is managing?"

In the bathroom, there appeared to be more water on the floor than in the tub as Lily splashed away amid the suds and floating toys. Richard stood up to join Jane and me in the doorway. His sleeves were rolled up, the front of his shirt soaked.

Jane touched his cheek affectionately. "Business as usual?" She seemed to have forgotten her sharp words from earlier.

I noticed that Lily was holding the toy dog with the bobbing head. "No, Lily," I said. "Don't put that in the water."

"She won't let go of it," Richard said.

Jane leaned in closer. "What *is* it?"

"I bought it," I said quickly. "Today, when we were out."

"Where did you go?" Jane asked.

I hesitated, unsure how to respond.

"A walk!" Lily said.

I stared at her, amazed.

"That's nice," Jane said. "Did you have a nice walk today
with Hua, Lily?"

Lily nodded, looking not at her mother but at me. I felt like
hugging her with joy and gratitude, but when I crouched by
the tub, she walloped me with a huge splash. I laughed and
gently splashed her back. Dimly I was aware of Jane and Richard standing in the doorway, watching us. Maybe they, too,
were smiling.

Chapter Eight

The sound of crying drifted across the playground. I was sitting on the bench in the park near Greenwich and Jane, as I had throughout the spring and summer. The park looked different now; leaves drooped on the branches as though waiting for release, and the sunlight was thick and heavy. In my mind I was no longer an outsider, but just another woman who looked after a child. Lily had changed, too, and not only because I watched her movements with a different kind of attention. While a few months ago she had played by herself, now she was interacting with some of the other children, exchanging toys and playing in the sandbox with them. These other children, whom before I had regarded with distant interest or amusement, now made me nervous. Who knew what Lily might catch from them?

The crying was coming from where Lily and another little girl of about the same age were playing in the shade of a tree. Something had happened between them, but I couldn't tell what. I didn't even know who had started it, because the moment I glanced in their direction, the girl who hadn't been crying started to bawl louder than the other one. Their voices sounded remarkably alike, entwining in a wail that seemed to have shape as well as volume.

I reached the two little girls at the same time a young woman did. Although I could tell she was this child's mother rather than her nanny—they had the same white-blond hair and blue eyes—this woman looked like a student in her jeans with ragged holes at the knees and a tight faded T-shirt. Her hair was pulled back in a ponytail and her eyes were distorted behind a pair of very thick, black, plastic-rimmed glasses. I glanced at her daughter and hoped the father had good eyesight, otherwise this girl would be blind by the time she started school.

"What happened, Chloe?" the young woman asked her daughter. "Did you bite again?"

Alarmed, I pulled Lily to me and checked for teeth marks. "She bites?"

Chloe's mother grinned. "Yeah, she bites everybody. Just like a puppy." She looked around the playground and whispered, "Honestly, if she does it to one more kid here, some mother is going to sue."

"I won't tell."

"Great, thanks. Does your child bite?"

I looked at Lily, who was struggling to be released so she could join her biting friend. I straightened her skirt and let go of her. "No, my child does not bite." The words flowed smooth and confident from my mouth.

"I don't know why Chloe does it. All the child-care books I've read say they're supposed to have outgrown it by now. Maybe it's because she gets too much protein. Or maybe she gets too little protein. I don't know. My, that's a pretty dress your daughter's wearing. Chloe would have that stained or torn within five minutes. She doesn't care much about clothes. Who knows where she gets that from, right?"

I looked from Chloe's grubby overalls to her mother's outfit and we both laughed. Soon I learned that Chloe's mother had just moved to New York from Oregon so that her husband could start a graduate program in biology. She was an artist, but she'd given up painting when she found out she was pregnant with Chloe. She thought the turpentine would damage Chloe's brain development. Now she stayed home all day with Chloe in university housing, experimenting with recipes and trying to teach Chloe French in order to get into the right preschool.

"I don't think it's good for them to be in school before the age of three, do you?" Chloe's mother said.

"Definitely not," I said.

"But the aural centers of their brain should be stimulated, shouldn't they?"

"Of course."

It was easy to agree with what Chloe's mother thought or didn't think about child rearing. She seemed to have read a lot of books on the subject and I had the feeling she approached motherhood like her husband might one of his research projects.

"What's your daughter's name?"

"Lily."

"That's a lovely name. Chloe didn't have a name until two weeks after she was born. I had all these meat cravings so I thought she'd be a boy. Then I was in labor for almost *twenty-four* hours, so the last thing I was thinking of after she came out was what we should name her. Worst pain *in my life*. Thank God for epidurals, right?"

I nodded, even though I didn't know what she was talking about.

"For days after that I felt like my insides were going to fall out if I even coughed. My husband was totally grossed out by all of it. You'd think that he wouldn't be so squeamish after dissecting lab rats all day, but he was. Hey, what does *your* husband do?"

I could have made something up, but the thought of a husband made my mind reel. "No husband," I said.

Chloe's mother clapped her hands to her mouth. "Oh my God. I am so sorry. I shouldn't have assumed there was a man in the picture at all. Did I forget what year it is already?"

"It's okay."

"No, it is *not* okay." Chloe's mother shook her head so hard that her ponytail snapped back and forth. "The whole *point* is that the traditional mother-father paradigm no longer exists in families. My husband and I know gay parents with adopted kids, straight couples with adopted kids, lesbian parents with natural kids, straight couples with adopted *and* natural kids . . . the permutations are endless." She paused to take a breath. "Hey, look." She nodded at Lily and Chloe, who had been playing quietly together with Lily's doll—most likely the source of the biting and crying before—while we had been talking. "They seem to be getting along pretty well."

I nodded.

"Really well. I mean, usually Chloe would be biting again by now. Hey, do you want to arrange a playdate or something?"

"What is this *playdate*?" I remembered encountering the word before in Jane's schedule book.

"You know, we arrange a time when the kids can come over and play at your place or my place. One-on-one social interaction is very important at this age."

There was no possibility Chloe could come over to Jane and Richard's apartment without the truth about me being revealed. "No! I mean to say . . . I don't think it is good for Lily."

Chloe's mother blinked behind her thick glasses, which just seemed to magnify her hurt and confusion. "Oh. Okay, then." We didn't speak for a while. Then she rose stiffly and said, "Chloe and I should be going home now anyway. See you around the park."

"See you." I looked after them as they left, Chloe hoisted capably on her mother's hip.

Though I never found out her name, I had liked Chloe's mother. I'd felt more friendliness toward her during our short interaction than anyone I had met in America since Ah Jing. Perhaps because we were around the same age, and she had talked to me like I was an equal, which she had truthfully believed I was. She hadn't asked where I had come from or when I had come to this country or if I had been to Chinatown. Other than assuming Lily was my daughter, she hadn't even seemed to notice that I was Chinese. I wonder if things would have been different if I had said from the beginning that I was Lily's nanny. Maybe she would have decided I wasn't worth talking to. Maybe she would have acted the same way toward me. I suspected that it wouldn't have mattered.

I looked at Lily, who also seemed a little sad that she had lost her playmate.

"Never mind, Lily," I said. "We don't need them. It's just you"—I poked her tummy, making her giggle—"and me."

"You," she repeated, reaching up to poke my stomach, "and me." She poked herself and fell backward onto the ground.

Laughing, I picked her up and tucked her head underneath my chin. She smelled sweet and sour—like the banana she had eaten earlier for a snack, and dirt and grass from the playground, and her soft, fine hair that should have been washed the night before. It was more comforting than any perfume.

~ ~ ~

Because I didn't want to run into Chloe and her mother, I started going to the park later in the day. When I didn't see them again, I wondered if they had gone back to Oregon. Or if Chloe's mother had enrolled her in preschool after all and started painting again. Then I stopped thinking about them altogether and it seemed as if I had imagined our encounter.

Until then, I had never thought that while Lily was starting to play with other children in the park, I might become friends with someone there, too. But, for the most part, the other women seemed unapproachable. The more time I spent in the park, the more I noticed the various hierarchies within. True, we were all looking after children, but there were the few women who were obviously the mothers of their children, then the veteran nannies whom I recognized from last winter, and new younger nannies that gathered together in clusters related to their native languages. The presence of men was rare: the lone father taking care of a child, a husband dropping by to speak to a wife.

Jane took to stopping by the park on her way home from work, and then I would relinquish Lily into her care. She seemed overwhelmed with happiness to see Lily, as if they had been separated for days rather than hours. I hadn't considered that she might enjoy her time with Lily more if she had less of it.

Sometimes I'd stay in the park after they left, watching as nanny after nanny collected the children to take back to their real parents. When they were gone the park was transformed into a different space, silent and empty except for people walking their dogs or cutting through on their way somewhere else.

One day, Jane was particularly late to pick up Lily. I was watching the gate when I saw her enter with a man who was not Richard. The two of them looked like a couple, though, with their heads bent toward each other as they talked. Even if this man weren't with Jane, even if he weren't in a park full of women and children, I think I would have noticed him. From a distance it was his height, his head of curly brown hair, his lanky limbs that made him look almost awkward. When he came closer, it was his eyes—the deep, dark brown of moist, rich soil—and the way the corners of his lips lifted in a grin, which would become imprinted, for some time, upon my memory. He moved past me and picked Lily up. She let him, which she never would have done with a stranger.

"She's gotten so big," he commented.

"Yes, she has, hasn't she?" Jane said. She widened her smile to include me. "Evan, this is Lily's nanny, Hua. She's from China."

Now the young man looked at me. "Nice to meet you." He set Lily down and extended his hand.

So this was the Evan in Jane's schedule book, the one she'd been having lunch dates with before the summer. The one that I'd imagined she'd been having an affair with, driving Richard mad.

Jane and Evan started talking about the museum, continuing a conversation that they'd obviously begun on their way to the park. They drifted away from the bench to a spot under a tree.

"Come here, Lily." I sat her down next to me on the bench so she wouldn't follow them.

"Read this." Lily pushed her book into my hands.

"Can you read it to me?" I suggested without looking at her, still keeping an eye on Jane and Evan.

"Once upon a time . . ." Lily started telling a story about a princess named Lily and her horse, although from what I remembered, the book was about a family of bears.

Beyond the singsong of Lily's voice, I couldn't quite make out what Jane and Evan were saying. But I could imagine the kind of endearments and hidden signals that might pass between them, in Jane's creamy eyelids when she looked down, in the brown line of Evan's throat when he threw back his head and laughed.

"The end." Lily shut the book and looked up at me, expectant.

"Very good," I told her.

Jane and Evan returned to the bench.

"Time to go home now," Jane said, taking Lily's hand. "Welcome back," she said to Evan.

"Welcome back yourself."

He patted Lily's head, gave me a nod, and then walked off. I wish I could say that my first encounter with Evan wasn't that ordinary, that we'd had an actual conversation, but there it was. There was really nothing about it, other than a few premature flutters in my stomach, more akin to food poisoning than infatuation.

"Who is he?" I asked Jane later.

"A coworker at the museum."

"That is all?" I realized what I was implying and added, "He is a friend?"

"Yes. He's been a pretty good friend to me over the years."

I asked Jane to tell me more about him, and she laughed. "Where do I begin? He used to be a student of mine when I taught a class on Tang Dynasty landscape painting. It was a great class, if I do say so myself, exclusively on *sanshui* painting. You know, mountain-sky—"

"Yes," I said. "I know."

"Well, this must have been, what, three or four years ago. Then, about the time Richard and I adopted Lily, he got an internship at the museum just as I was taking a leave of absence. We'd meet up every week for lunch and he'd tell me what was going on there. I probably knew too much about everyone when I went back.

"Not that he was a gossip," Jane added, as if afraid of giving me a bad impression. "Evan isn't malicious. He just seems to be able to see through people, right to what they want. He could tell that I was going to adopt a baby months before I told anyone, even my closest friends. He said that he could tell I wanted a baby, even when I couldn't admit it to myself. I don't know if that means he's crazy or I am."

"No," I said. "I can believe that."

I could believe, upon seeing Jane for the first time, that she appeared to be lacking something vital to her belief in herself. I don't know if I would have guessed it was a baby, but she had the look of someone who would always be wanting something. I was seeing it now as she talked about Evan, and again I wondered about their relationship.

"So you know each other well?" A delicate prod.

"Yes and no. I suppose he knows me better than I know him. I don't know much about him outside of class and work, what he does, who his other friends are. But for a while, after Lily came, I really had no one else I could talk to. I was away from work, I didn't know many other mothers, and my single friends are child free. He was probably the best friend I had then. We continued meeting until this summer, when he went away."

"Where did he go?"

"He was doing an intensive language course in Beijing. You should get him to tell you about it. I think you two have a lot in common."

I felt Jane had given me her blessing, though I didn't know for what.

~ ~ ~

She must have made the same sort of suggestion to Evan, because a few weeks later he accompanied her to the park again. After she and Lily left to go home, he stayed and sat down beside me. For a while we both sat in the tentative silence of two people trying to get to know each other.

"How did you know Jane wanted a baby?" I blurted out.

Evan laughed. "She told you that?"

"It's not true?"

"Well, it was a lucky guess. Also, Jane's assistant used to be late all the time because she had to wait for a babysitter for her five-year-old son. Jane was very understanding about that, always asking her how her kid was, concerned if he was sick, that kind of thing."

"What about Richard?" I asked.

"I don't think he wanted a child."

"What do you mean?" I thought about the times I had seen Richard playing with Lily, how she immediately ran to him when he came home from work.

"I don't know him that well, but he doesn't seem like a family man. He's very withdrawn, like the only thing that matters to him is his work. My father was like that."

"What did he do?"

"He was an artist. He had a studio in the city and he was always there, or out drinking with his artist buddies. They were his real family. Eventually he and my mother got divorced and he remarried. Whenever I saw him, he reminded me I was a disappointment. He never forgave me for studying art history instead of trying to become a painter like himself. He just couldn't accept that I was no good at it."

Evan gave me a half smile. "I don't know why I'm telling you this. I never tell anyone this. It's just easy to talk to you, I guess."

What I wanted most was for Evan to tell me what he thought of me, but I only said, "I like to listen." And I did. I could think of nothing I wanted to do more than to sit there in the park and listen to him telling me things he had never told any other girl, even if it was all about himself.

But he didn't say any more, and a silence fell between us. Then I remembered Jane's suggestion and asked, "What was your summer in Beijing like?"

"It was amazing. I thought it was going to be this sea of proletariats in blue Mao suits all chanting and waving their little red books, but it was just full of regular people. There were crowded buses and cars and taxis and pollution and everything we have here. Have you ever been to Beijing?"

I shook my head. I remembered as a child in school, whenever we were asked where we would most like to visit, the answer should always be the capital, Beijing. But few of us had ever gone. It was far in the north, a train ride of days, and none of us had ever been on an airplane.

"I guess that's not surprising," Evan said. "I haven't been to Washington, D.C., and I've lived on the East Coast all my life."

"Did you go to Tiananmen Square and see where Mao is buried?" I asked, breathless. This always topped the teacher-approved list of places we should want to see.

"The mausoleum? No, the line was too long and it was ninety degrees. We just watched the kids flying kites and, you know, tried to make the guards in front of the Hall of the People laugh. They sure are tough bastards."

I didn't smile, and the grin on his face faded. "Sorry. It's not right to make fun of a place like that, after what happened there. I mean, you can still see bullet holes in the concrete. I remember the student massacre from eighty-nine on television when I was a kid . . . What was it like where you were, when that happened? Jane said you're from the southeast of China?"

"We didn't know a lot. The news is—how to say—" I grasped at my fading English.

"Controlled by the government?"

"Yes."

I didn't say how I had woken in the middle of the night to see my grandmother listening to the radio, tears streaming silently down her face; how the next day everyone gathered on the streets as if in a dream, their faces like stone, as the radios broadcast that the ruffians who had attempted to cause unrest in the capital had been punished for the good of the people.

"What I want to know," Evan said, "is why people in China put up with news that is propaganda."

I shrugged. "Most people don't care. They are too busy working, trying to get enough to eat. Here, in America, there are so many newspapers and magazines telling different things, who knows what to believe?"

"Well, at least you have a choice here. In China there's just like that one party line. And it's everywhere you go." He jumped up, and for a moment I was afraid he was going to leave, but it was only to emphasize his next point. "Like when I visited Kashgar. So the people there are mostly Muslim, right? They don't even look Chinese."

I belatedly figured out what he was referring to, the city in western China that the Chinese called *Kashi*. It was on the Silk Road, practically on the border with Kazakhstan. I had seen pictures of the native people, and with their brown skin and long noses they looked more Central Asian than Han Chinese.

"So this city is full of mosques and bazaars, but still there's a statue of Mao in the park, facing west. You know, the one where he looks like this." Evan stood still for a moment, right hand outstretched.

"That statue is in many cities," I said.

"Exactly. It's everywhere! It's a symbol showing that even thousands of miles away from the capital the government still has control. Did you know that hundreds of people from the eastern part of the country are sent west every year, driving the local people out? They're tearing down the old buildings and replacing them so that Kashgar looks like any other modern city in China, but that statue is everywhere. You don't see that in America."

I thought for a moment. "What about McDonald's signs?"

He stopped pacing, which was a relief, because I was beginning to think he had some kind of nervous habit. "You have a point there."

"So what did you find amazing in Beijing?" I asked.

He sat down again. "So one day I wake up early and get on my bike, this ancient iron bike made from, like, melted-down pots or something. I start pedaling south, from the campus of my school in the Haidian district. The streets are full of other bike riders and buses, even donkeys and carts. There's all this dust and smoke flying around.

"Then suddenly the road I'm on is being fed into some larger road, and I'm in the middle of what seems like hundreds of bike riders going down Chang'an Avenue in front of Tiananmen Square. Everyone's going at the same slow pace, in perfect harmony, kind of like when you see those old folks doing tai chi in the parks. And you know what I felt?"

"What?" I hung on the edge of his pause, anticipating something wonderful.

"Absolute peace. *That* was amazing."

He looked at me with eyes that were intently, unnervingly brown. I wanted to turn away but I couldn't, as if I was watching a movie and was afraid of missing an important scene. I understood now what Jane had meant when she said Evan could see right through a person. Although here I couldn't tell if he just wanted to impress me with the sincerity of his gaze, or if there was something more behind it. Whatever it was, I could feel myself widening in front of him, opening up to something that made my breath come faster.

"I have to go now," I said faintly.

"It was nice talking to you," he said. "Maybe we can do it again sometime." He paused. "Actually, have you ever been to the Museum of Asian Art? Where Jane and I work?"

I shook my head.

"We can go this Friday if you want, after you're done baby-sitting. They're open late—"

I couldn't wait for him to finish. "Yes, please."

"Great. I'll meet you outside the museum at seven, then."

This time I could turn away from his smile. But on the way home the quickening in my heart remained, as if it were remembering something it had long tried to forget. Yes, this was how it had started with Teacher Zhang.

Chapter Nine

In the beginning of my third and last year in college, I felt like anything could happen. I was doing well at school, so well that I was sure I would graduate at the top of my class. I was best friends with Swallow, whose family was wealthier and more important than any other girl's at school. After I graduated, I could use my English skills to work for a foreign import-export company, or find a job in Shanghai, or even try for one of the scholarships that sent students to America to continue their studies. Whatever it held, my future looked promising. But what happened with Teacher Zhang changed all that.

Until the incident with *Anna Karenina,* Teacher Zhang had not seemed to take any notice of me in class. Afterward, he did not pay any attention to me for a long time. Then one afternoon, as I was going back to the classroom to pick up a book I had forgotten, he called my name across the empty courtyard.

"Miss Wu!"

I blushed at hearing him call me outside of class.

"Your English is fairly good, isn't it? Your oral English teacher speaks quite highly of you."

I colored further at the thought of teachers talking about students behind our backs. "I suppose so."

"I was wondering, perhaps would you like to borrow my English version of *Anna Karenina?*"

Of course I did.

"I can bring it to class next time. Or, I have a better idea, why don't you come with me now back to my apartment and pick it up? It's not far. Or do you have to stay behind?"

I shook my head. Something should have alerted me to the inappropriateness of my decision, but I was too dazzled by Teacher Zhang's attentions. I let him guide me out of the gate to a path that led behind the school grounds. I was aware that we were walking side by side—not close enough to touch, but it did more to increase the thumping of my heart than if there had been actual physical contact.

The other young teachers at school were female so they lived in a dormitory on campus, the same as the students. Those who had husbands or families lived in school-subsidized housing close by. But because Teacher Zhang was unmarried and a man, he was given special treatment. He had his own apartment at the military academy not far from our school. It was a pleasant walk, up a path of stone steps cut into the hill. When I looked back I could see the Min River glittering below, like a necklace strung through the trees.

Teacher Zhang's apartment was about the size of the dorm room I shared with seven other girls, and in not much better shape. Plaster peeled from the ceiling, and the wall behind the two-burner stove was scorched black from too many cooking fires. Books lay haphazardly on shelves made from planks of wood. Teacher Zhang invited me to sit down on the single chair in front of the desk. I was glad he had offered me the chair. There was nowhere else to sit except the bed, which looked like a student's with its blue iron frame and threadbare blanket. That would have been improper.

He offered me tea and cursed softly when he discovered the thermos was empty. "The woman who cleans must have forgotten to bring hot water this morning," he said. "I'll go get some."

After he closed the door behind him, the strange situation I was in dawned upon me. I was alone in my male teacher's room without anyone else knowing about it. I stared at the green linoleum floor tiles beneath my feet, and the map of the world above the desk across from me. Then I felt bold enough to get up and look at the bookshelves, where there were many books in English and French.

"Do you know how to read French, too?" I exclaimed when Teacher Zhang returned with the hot water.

He shook tea leaves from a canister into two blue-patterned mugs. "Yes, I learned it in Shanghai, at the teacher's college."

That greatly impressed me. I had never known anyone who had lived in Shanghai before, and the city was as glamorous to me as London or New York.

"What was Shanghai like?" I asked.

He handed me a mug. "Well, I'll tell you."

In between his stories about walking on the Bund along the Pearl River and listening to jazz at the famed Peace Hotel, I became comfortable with Teacher Zhang. By the end of the afternoon I forgot to take his copy of *Anna Karenina*, the reason I had come to his apartment in the first place.

In class, things remained the same. Teacher Zhang didn't call on me, and I never raised my hand to speak again. But after school, it was different. Now we would meet at the foot of the path alongside the Min River instead of on the school grounds because it was too risky. We talked about books and our favorite writers, but I enjoyed hearing about his college life in Shanghai the most.

"Why did you leave Shanghai?" I asked once. "It sounds so exciting."

"It *was* exciting. But I grew up there. No place you grow up in stays exciting for long. I was tired of big city life. Well, obviously not tired enough to go teach peasants in some country school. I'm not idealistic like Tolstoy's Levin."

I laughed. He handed me my mug of tea as usual and sat down on the bed beside me.

"I would like to go back to the big city someday. But not Shanghai. Maybe Paris. Study at a foreign university. Where do you want to go?"

I looked at the map of the world on the wall across from us, the same map that could be found in any schoolroom in the country. China was in the middle of it, as befit its name in Chinese—*zhongguo,* the middle kingdom. It was only later that I realized that if you were in America, then America was in the middle of the map. I supposed it changed depending on what country you were in. But back then, China was the center of the world for me.

"I can't go anywhere," I said.

"Of course you can. You're smart enough. There are scholarships they give out to study in America. You could apply."

I shook my head. "I can't leave my grandmother."

"What about your parents?"

I told him about my parents' death, growing up with my grandmother, the Western-style house my grandparents used to own. I had told no one else how I felt about these things, not even Swallow. Teacher Zhang listened and was kind, so kind that, in the end, when he placed his hand over mine, I didn't move away. I turned my palm up and our fingers interlaced. We sat there, holding hands, for what seemed like the rest of the afternoon. That night I could still feel his touch.

The next day, when I reached the part of the riverbank where I usually waited for Teacher Zhang, I didn't stop. I continued walking, past the bridge and the green sheds where the fishermen kept their boats. When the day turned to evening, my feet led me to Teacher Zhang's door. He opened it at my knock and appeared surprised to see me.

"Can I come in?" I asked.

"If I let you come in—" He looked very serious. "You know what you are doing, don't you?"

"Yes," I said. I took his hand and placed it underneath my blouse and over my heart so that he would also know.

~ ~ ~

Since Teacher Zhang, my heart hadn't stirred. Now, if what I was feeling for Evan wasn't exactly a schoolgirl crush, it was something very much like it. Since I had met him, I found it more difficult to breathe when I heard his name mentioned, and sometimes I would wake up in the middle of the night with the abashed suspicion that I had just been dreaming about him. But I also had to remind myself that this situation was different from what I had experienced as a schoolgirl. Evan and I didn't have to hide, and we had Jane's approval.

Perhaps that was what mattered to me most, that Jane seemed to want us to be together. I began to think she had brought Evan to the park specifically for me. Certainly, she had encouraged us to speak to each other, and she left us alone so we could do so. She had decided that I would be good for him, just as she had decided that I should be the one to take care of Lily. I was honored that she had chosen me, yet again.

Chapter Ten

The Museum of Asian Art was a steel and glass construction that reflected the sky. It looked much like any other building in that part of town, except a banner hung over the facade proclaiming the latest exhibit: The Lotus Position. Below the words, against the red background, sat a twenty-foot-high golden Buddha. Its customary blank smile stretched from one side of the banner to the other, reminding me of pictures I had seen of giant Buddhas carved into the sides of mountains.

Beneath the banner were groups of tourists and the occasional solitary person like myself, waiting for someone to show up. I had hurried uptown from the park that afternoon as soon as Jane had arrived. I hadn't told her where I was going, but I thought I saw something mischievous in the smile she gave me as I was leaving. As if she'd had a hand in setting up this date.

I thought of Evan's invitation to the museum as a date, although I had no way of knowing if it really was one. My relationship with Teacher Zhang had started over books, and very few of my classmates had dated, even though we were in college. Our teachers told us that our studies came first, not dreaming about boys. The few girls who dated did so secretly without the teachers or their parents knowing. And when they came to class with eyes red from crying, the rest of us would both pity and envy them. Back then, I had no idea how dates operated in America. I knew only the images from movies: high schoolers necking in the backseats of cars.

Earlier that day, before taking Lily to the park, I had walked restlessly through the apartment. I looked through Jane's closet, remembering the stylish outfits she wore when she went out on Saturday nights with Richard. I had no time that afternoon to go back to the boardinghouse to change, even if I'd had anything worth changing into. If I had been Jane's size, I might have snuck something of hers underneath my own clothes. But, lucky for her, I was too short. So I applied some of her makeup and splashed her perfume around my neck, which I hoped she hadn't noticed as I left her and Lily.

Walking down the street toward the subway stop, I had passed a couple heading in the opposite direction. They looked oddly familiar. I glanced over my shoulder and saw them turn down Jane and Richard's street. Then I realized they were the couple who lived in the apartment across the air shaft, the ones I had seen engaged in quite an intimate activity the first night I had babysat Lily. I hadn't recognized them because they were clothed. A warmth spread through my body, lingering in places that I was embarrassed to be still thinking about as I waited in front of the museum.

"Hey," said a voice by my ear. Evan had arrived.

We went into the building and stopped at the admissions desk. Evan knew some of the people who worked there, and after speaking to them, he gestured for me to precede him into the museum. I was impressed that we didn't have to buy tickets.

It was cold inside the museum, and the lighting was low except for brief bursts that illuminated cases of objects and small framed drawings on the walls. The first case contained embroidered satin slippers that had been worn by women with bound feet. The shoes looked more fit for the hooves of animals than humans. I remembered that my grandmother had once told me how her mother, my great-grandmother, had tried to bind my grandmother's feet when she was a girl. It had been so painful that she'd cried the entire day, and her mother had relented and allowed her feet to grow.

In the second case were objects that I couldn't figure out the use of at first. They were cylinders of stone or amber or jade, rounded and tapered at one end, ranging in size from my littlest finger to a cucumber. After I moved to the first drawing, I understood what those objects were supposed to represent and how they were supposed to be used. A flush spread over my face. I looked at Evan, who seemed not to notice and was looking at the items on display with a studious expression. I glanced at the sign by the entrance that described the exhibit: The Lotus Position: Sexual Practices and Proclivities in Ancient China.

The drawing that had clued me in to the nature of my surroundings depicted a woman lying on her back in a bamboo grove, unclothed except for the shoes on her dainty feet. Behind her crouched a man with an open robe and exposed phallus. Both the man and woman looked faintly amused, as if they had just heard a funny but not particularly dirty joke. The card beside it read: In the Soaring Dragon position, the man places his jade stem inside of the woman's jade gate. . . .

"How are you liking it?" Evan asked.

"Um . . . it is very interesting," I murmured, glad that the dim lighting hid my face.

As we walked past more of these drawing—depicting the Playful Monkeys position, Floating Tortoises position, and Flying Phoenixes position—I became less flustered and more fascinated. How strange it was that no matter where they were, in a teahouse or the woods or on a horse, the couple always wore the same expressions of mild interest. With their moon faces and white limbs, they looked like wax dolls. The woman always kept her shoes on. In one drawing, there was a third person, a servant of indeterminate sex but with the same pleasant facial expression. The servant was bent over, providing a back for his or her mistress to lean on while the master thrust away.

"Look, that's the spotter," Evan whispered, indicating the servant.

"What's that?" I whispered back.

"It's the person who watches to make sure you don't drop something and hurt yourself. You know, in weight lifting . . . oh, never mind."

"There are many . . . um . . . positions," I commented.

"Yeah, who knew people back then could be so randy. Actually, these drawings date from the Tang Dynasty, and the Tang Dynasty emperors were notorious for their sexual decadence. . . ."

I half listened as Evan told me bits of Chinese history, some of which I guessed he had learned from Jane's class.

Back outside on the glittering street in front of the museum it was dark. My heart fell when I thought our date was over, then lifted when Evan asked if I was hungry. Of course I was. He suggested that we go to a place nearby to eat; he thought I would like it.

As we walked down the street, I noticed that the suited men and women from earlier that evening had been replaced by couples heading out for a night on the town. The men wore open-necked shirts, their hair brushed back to fall neatly against their collars. The women, in dresses with low necks and high hemlines, clutched their shiny purses with one hand and the arms of their dates with the other as they navigated the cracks of the sidewalk in high heels. The area that we were approaching was full of these couples. They stood outside doorways, light and vibrant sound spilling over them. More stepped out of taxis that pulled up to the curb. I stood still, bewildered by the sudden crowd, until Evan placed a hand at my back and steered me into a restaurant.

The first thing I saw was a huge gold Buddha, not unlike the one pictured on the banner in front of the museum, above my head in the foyer. The interior of the restaurant reminded me of the museum, too, with its elegant chill and dim lighting. But this place was noisy with the low-pitched murmur of collective voices, punctuated by some kind of fast beat.

I followed a waitress through the press of people to a low table in a corner of the room. It was so dark that all I could see of anyone else was the occasional white shirt cuff or gleam of jewelry. Small lights set below the cavernous ceiling exposed more gold Buddhas that grinned down on us.

Evan asked me something and I had to lean in so close that his lips almost touched my ear.

"Do you want something to drink?"

I looked at the indecipherable menu, then shrugged to indicate my helplessness. Evan beckoned a waitress over, whispered something to her. In a moment she returned with two martini glasses of a pinkish liquid. I took a cautious sip. A sweetness slid smoothly down my throat, followed by a bitter burn.

"Do you like it?"

He looked so expectant that I nodded, even though my empty stomach recoiled at the sweet-bitter combination.

"What is it?"

"A lychee cosmo."

I recognized the lychee part. Looking through the rest of the menu, a few familiar words jumped out at me—duck, mushroom, bamboo shoot—but there were others that I didn't recognize, like carpaccio, granita, and julienned. It was as if someone had taken the menu from a Chinese restaurant and translated it into another language.

"What kind of food is this?" I asked.

"Chinese mostly, but some Thai, Burmese, and Vietnamese, too. It's a bit of everything. It's called Asian fusion."

"Asian confusion?" I asked, thinking I had misheard him.

Evan laughed. "Something like that. Order anything you want."

I slid the menu over to him. "You choose."

Looking around, I noticed the waitresses were wearing some variation of a *qipao* in black satin embroidered with gold. But with their Western women's bodies, the style looked all wrong, emphasizing the bumps of their hips and breasts, whereas a *qipao* was supposed to make the lines of a woman's body long and lithe. The slits on the sides of the dresses revealed black high-heeled boots that went up to the thigh. Old Chou at the Lucky Duck would never have allowed his waitresses to wear something so provocative. These outfits reminded me of what some restaurant hostesses in China wore when they stood outside of places that advertised private rooms with karaoke. My grandmother always walked past them with an air of disdain, as if they were prostitutes.

Suddenly all of the waitresses in the room reminded me of prostitutes. I hoped Jane had not told Evan what my previous job had been. I would rather die than admit to him now that I had been a waitress. I glanced around the room again and told myself I was now a customer, and in the dark I looked as sophisticated as any of them. I took another sip of my drink, and this time the bitterness was pleasant. My head was beginning to feel light, as if it might fly off my shoulders.

The food came, but I barely tasted anything. My stomach's memory seemed to soak it up as fast as I swallowed it. I finished my drink and Evan ordered me another. The room grew hot and close, and the chatter of voices unbearable. I excused myself to go use the bathroom. As I passed the mirror on my way to a toilet stall, I was surprised to see that my face was very pink, as if I had just walked into a room full of real-life couples engaging in various animal-named positions and was mortified beyond belief. I rushed past my reflection into a stall to throw up.

Within seconds, everything I had just eaten had come into the world again. I knelt on the floor, gripping the edges of the toilet, until the spasms in my stomach subsided. The harsh fluorescent lights bouncing off the tiles hurt my eyes. Although I could still feel the muffled beat of the music, the bathroom was quiet enough so that I could hear ringing in my ears. Then I heard a delicate cough. My gaze slid over the floor to the next stall, to a pair of red shoes with heels that looked as if they could puncture someone's heart. The shoes left the stall and tapped over to the sink. I waited, not wanting to reveal myself, but after a few minutes I knew I was not going to be left alone. I flushed the toilet and emerged sheepishly.

"Are you okay?"

An Asian woman in a red halter top and slinky black pants was standing in front of a sink, applying lipstick the shade of her shoes. Her hair was pulled back from her face in a ponytail that curled against the side of her neck like a black snake. I met her eyes in the mirror and nodded.

"Fresh off the boat?"

Now I could detect the slight accent in her voice. She dropped the tube of lipstick into her purse and dug around in it.

"Hold out your hand," she said and dropped a tiny white pill into my palm. Then she took an empty martini glass someone had left behind on the counter, rinsed and filled it with water from the sink, and gave it to me. "Here. You look like you could use some cheering up."

I stared at the pill, then at her face. She looked so kind, so comforting. She looked like she had been through all of this before. I gulped the pill down and, almost immediately, I did feel better.

The woman smiled again and brushed past me through the door. When I emerged seconds later, I had lost sight of her. Back in the noisy restaurant, I felt I had dreamed the whole thing.

When I returned to our table, Evan said, "I went ahead and ordered dessert. I didn't know what you wanted so I got a bunch of stuff. Green-tea brulee, jasmine-chocolate tart, taro-lavender cheesecake. . . ."

My appetite was back, and so was the lightness in my head, but now it felt like my entire body was floating. Evan was talking to me, but I let his voice drift into the background. Every so often he'd touch my hand to get my attention or brush a wisp of hair back from my face, and my senses were so fired up when he did that I could barely sit still. The check came.

I let Evan take care of it and leaned back into the red-and-gold cushions, feeling like that was the only way I could keep from leaving the ground.

Outside, Evan hailed a cab. He asked me where I should be dropped off and I said the first address that popped into my head.

"That can't be right," he said. "That's where Jane lives. Where do *you* live?"

I repeated the address and laughed at the puzzled look on his face.

Finally he gave up and told the cabdriver his own address. We rocketed down busy streets, a wash of color and lights pouring through the window. Evan's arm was around me, keeping me upright. I leaned into his side and hung on. I had never seen the city at this time of night. The clusters of people at the corners, the signs of bars and clubs, were like part of a new and different world. I didn't know whether I was on the East Side or West Side, downtown or uptown, and it didn't matter.

The moment I stepped out of the cab it was if my bones had turned to jelly. Evan had to help me up what seemed like dozens of flights of stairs. The front door of his apartment opened directly into the kitchen, which had a shower stall next to the sink. Evan led me into another room and made me sit down on a worn leather couch. He pressed a glass of water into my hand.

"Feeling better?" He sat beside me.

I nodded and managed to place the glass on the coffee table without spilling it. The room looked like a student's with its unmade bed and piles of books. A few posters of Hong Kong gangster movies decorated the walls and I stared at them, mesmerized by the patterns and colors.

"What are you thinking?" Evan asked.

I smiled sleepily. "It is a nice place."

He shrugged. "It's small but the rent's decent. I've been living in this neighborhood for years. It's the only place I know of in Manhattan where you can get an empanada and a good German beer at two in the morning."

I stood up and made my way toward the bookshelves. I recognized some Asian art history books like the ones in Jane's living room, books on Far Eastern religion, screenplays by Hong Kong film directors, a Chinese dictionary. A translation of *Dream of the Red Chamber*.

"You read this?" I asked, taking the volume down.

"No, I tried but didn't get too far."

I picked up one of Mao's little red books, displayed on a shelf along with several Communist-era buttons and pins.

"A souvenir from Beijing," Evan explained. "They were being sold everywhere on the street, and not only to tourists. I was told that a decade ago no one wanted them and now they're collectors' items."

Next to those things on the shelf was a penknife that didn't look very Asian. It had the words Niagara Falls engraved on it.

"What is this?" I asked, holding up the knife.

"Oh, that. Another souvenir. From a trip my family took when I was ten. I pretty much keep everything."

I moved on down the bookcase to some framed photos: a kind-looking, middle-aged couple that I assumed were Evan's parents, and a young woman with Evan's brown eyes standing by herself in a graduation cap and gown.

"That's my sister. She graduated from college last year."

I paused at the next photo. A young woman was standing in a park, her long hair pulled gracefully over one shoulder. The picture was not very good and her face was shaded, but you could tell she was smiling. She looked Chinese.

"Who is that?"

Evan cleared his throat. "Julie, my ex-girlfriend. We broke up before I left for Beijing."

"She was born here?" There was something about her smile that reminded me of the pictures of my Uncle George and Aunt May's daughters that I had seen at their house in New Jersey.

"Yes. Her parents came from Taiwan. She doesn't speak any Chinese."

"She's very pretty," I said. I heard a rustle from the couch, a creak of released springs.

"You're very pretty," Evan said.

He kissed me, leaning me into the bookcase so that I could feel the spines of the books against my back. I obediently opened my mouth and his tongue filled it. I closed my eyes and it seemed even bigger.

"Mmmm," he said into my neck. "You smell good, too."

I had put on Jane's perfume earlier. "What do I smell like?"

"Fresh. Clean. Like my first girlfriend."

Many Julies ago, I thought.

His hands moved up underneath my shirt and drew me toward him so that I could feel him pressed against my thigh. It wasn't far to his bed; the room was so small that he merely had to turn me to the right like a practiced dancer and I fell straight onto it. Although the room wasn't cold, I shivered as Evan removed my clothes. He ran a hand down my neck, pausing for a moment over the goose-fleshed nipple of my left breast, before sliding to my waist.

"You're so tiny," he whispered, and pushed his hand between my legs. His fingers came away slick, but he wet them in his mouth anyway and slid them inside me. I gasped, tightening my thighs around his wrist. "Relax," he said. "I'll be back in a moment."

He moved away and I closed my eyes. I heard a dresser drawer open and close, the unbuckling of a belt, the unzipping of a fly, the smack of rubber against skin. Then he was above me, one hand pushing my legs farther apart while the other gripped himself.

"Um," he said after a moment. "The jade stem is having some trouble entering the jade gate."

I giggled.

"Want to give me a hand?"

"Okay."

He guided my hand to his sheathed penis. My fingers closed around it, and it warmed and twitched and grew. He gently moved my hand aside and proceeded to enter the jade gate. At first it felt as futile as someone trying to fit a hand into a too-small glove. Then something in me gave up all resistance. I touched his body with curiosity, the oddness of the hair on his chest, the smooth planes of his shoulders, as if this were something wondrous and new.

Of course it wasn't entirely new. I shut my eyes and tried to remember the one other time I had allowed someone so close to me. The losing of myself in the warm breath of another. The bittersweet pain, and then the unbearable sense of shame that had followed. Teacher Zhang's eyes when he closed the door behind me and I was left in the chilly evening. The memory drew me deep into myself and then pushed me out with such force that I was left trembling like I had been spat out from the sea onto a cold shore. Evan collapsed on top of me with what seemed like far less feeling. Then he raised himself up on one elbow and kissed my forehead.

"Did anyone ever tell you how nice and tight you are?"

When I didn't reply, he asked, "Are you okay? Do you want to clean up?" He indicated the shower stall in the kitchen.

I stayed in there for a long time, willing the hot water to beat the memory of Teacher Zhang from my skin. But I could still remember how I had felt, the ache of my body that faded much faster than the ache in my heart.

When I finally emerged from the shower and went into the other room, Evan was asleep. He stirred when I sat down on the bed and moved over so that I could lie down next to him. He draped an arm over me and fell asleep again. But I couldn't let myself do the same. I had never slept in the same bed as another person, except for Swallow when I stayed over at her house, and that wasn't the same. I couldn't relax.

After our one time together, Teacher Zhang was unable to look me in the eyes. He made me promise not to tell anyone what we had done. I knew he could lose his job if the truth got out, and I would be expelled from school. But I didn't have anyone to tell—my classmates wouldn't have believed me—and, furthermore, I would not have been able to describe what had happened even if I were asked. Our teachers had never told us about the physical relations between a man and a woman, except that we would find out after we were married and that it would hurt, so we shouldn't be eager to try it before then. It *had* hurt, but most of the time I had felt so detached from what was going on that it was as if I were watching myself and Teacher Zhang from the back of a classroom with a kind of vacant curiosity.

From then on, my relationship with Teacher Zhang was as if we had never shared any intimacy at all, not even that of borrowing and discussing books. I continued to wait at the river after school for him, but he started taking a different route home. In class, he refused to look in my direction. Sometimes, in a moment of quiet when we were working at our desks, I would catch his gaze resting on me over the bent heads of the other girls. When he saw me looking back at him, he would turn away as if he had glanced upon something bright and painful. Then, before the end of the semester, he left school, taking our secret with him.

Finally the darkness outside the window started to lift. Carefully I slid out from Evan's unconscious arms and got dressed. My hair was still wet, and I rubbed it dry while standing in front of the bookcase, looking at the picture of his ex-girlfriend. Now her smile seemed triumphant, as if she knew something that I didn't. Behind me, Evan turned over in bed. I had only a second to decide what to take. I grabbed the penknife that lay on a shelf nearby and slipped it into my pocket.

"Are you going?" he murmured.

"Yes."

"Okay. I'll call you."

I had closed the door behind me and was halfway down the stairs before I realized that he didn't have my number.

Outside, in the gritty pink of sunrise, I found myself on an empty street lined with old tenements. Even if I had been completely sober on the cab ride here, I wouldn't have recognized where I was. All the windows were dark except for those of a deli on the corner, and a vagrant was passed out in one of the doorways. I could be anywhere in the city.

I walked to the end of the street and turned south. Within a few minutes I passed Sara D. Roosevelt Park and was in Chinatown. I hadn't known all night that I was less than ten blocks from where I lived.

Part IV

Chapter Eleven

Lily seemed to know that I was upset in those days. I felt that she noticed how disappointed I was when Jane entered the park alone, how I would pretend I hadn't expected anyone else to be with her. She saw how I would look up every time a man walked by the gate. She studied my face, pale from lack of sleep, and would place her hands on each of my cheeks and pull to make me smile.

I didn't understand why I hadn't heard from Evan since that evening at the museum and what had followed after. True, even if he had known my number at the boardinghouse, there was no guarantee Mrs. Ma would be home to answer the telephone in the hall and slide a message under my door. But he knew where I worked during the day, and he knew where I was every afternoon. If he wanted to, he could ask Jane for my telephone number or how I was doing. Apparently, he never bothered.

Sometimes, at night, in my boardinghouse room, I'd hold the penknife I'd stolen from Evan's apartment. I'd put it on the windowsill next to the white pebble I had taken from the Templeton-Walkers' apartment the first time I'd babysat Lily. I'd press the smooth metal tip of the knife against my skin, against the parts of my body that Evan had touched. I imagined him as the ten-year-old boy who had purchased it as a souvenir alongside his younger sister and parents, an American family on vacation. Once I pressed so hard that a dot of blood appeared. I touched it with my thumb and brought it to my mouth.

I never knew whether Jane had guessed what had happened between Evan and me. She did seem to mention him less, while I hungered to hear anything about him. I doubted he would have told her, knowing that I worked for her. But sometimes I wanted to tell. The agony in my heart was sometimes such that I thought it would burst. I would listen to Jane's instructions about what not to let Lily eat before naptime, and answer her questions about the progress Lily was making in sharing her toys, all the while feeling like I would explode with words.

~ ~ ~

"Are there any special things that people do in China to celebrate birthdays?" Jane asked me one afternoon. "Lily is going to be three in November, and I'd like to throw her a party."

"There are some special foods," I said. "Long-life noodles and eggs." I knew that in America children received presents, but on my birthday my grandmother always prepared a bowl of noodles topped by two hard-boiled eggs, which represented the zeros in the number one hundred.

"No sweets or anything?"

I shook my head.

"Then I guess it'll have to be a combination of both cultures. We can't have a birthday without C-A-K-E." She looked meaningfully at where Lily was sitting at the kitchen table, drawing on a piece of paper with crayons. "Is there anything else?"

I thought hard. "When a baby is one hundred days old, the parents have a red-egg-and-ginger party."

"What's that?"

"Boiled eggs that are dyed red and pickled gingerroot that is also dyed red. It is for good luck. I can get it in Chinatown."

"That would be nice. I think it's safe to say that Lily didn't get to have that party when she was a baby, so we'll do it now. It's very important that this party shows Lily how special she is, how much we both love her."

I heard a twist in Jane's normally cheerful voice at that last part. She sounded regretful, more so than just at the idea that Lily might have missed her real red-egg-and-ginger party. Belatedly I realized she must mean not how much she and I loved Lily, but herself and Richard.

But the moment had passed. Jane was craning her neck to see what Lily had drawn. "That's a lovely abstract drawing, sweetie."

I turned to see, too. On the paper was a brown blob floating above a green scribble.

"It's a doggie. I want a doggie for my birthday."

"Lily, we already have a kitty," Jane pointed out. "Don't you like our kitty?"

"No, I want a doggie. Erin has a doggie."

"The Paulsons," Jane explained to me. "We visited them and their daughter Erin a couple of weekends ago."

It occurred to me that even though I spent over five hours a day, every weekday, with Lily, there were aspects of her life that I knew nothing about. I didn't know who she played with on the weekends, the children whose parents were friends of Jane and Richard. Although I was sometimes allowed to give

Lily her bath, I was not involved in the most fundamental activities of her life, like preparing her dinner or putting her to bed. I wasn't there to comfort her if she woke up in the middle of the night from a bad dream.

"Oh, I almost forgot," Jane continued. "I set up a playdate with Erin's mother for next Tuesday afternoon. You can have that day off."

"Thank you," I said. But I was trying to think of what I would do with myself that day. While working at the restaurant, I'd never had an entire weekday off. I couldn't go to the park as I had before I'd started babysitting Lily. Nor did I want to spend more time in the boardinghouse or in Chinatown, or even taking a walk to the water as I used to do when I had first arrived in America. Those days were over for me now.

~   ~   ~

That Tuesday I stood in front of the entrance to the Museum of Asian Art where Jane and Evan worked. I tried not to think about the emotions that I had felt the last time I'd been there, the heady anticipation for my date. I stayed away from the museum workers who were outside smoking, and hovered near a group of Japanese tourists, figuring that I'd blend in better that way.

After several minutes I saw Jane exit the glass doors. She looked around as if searching for someone, but fortunately her eyes passed over the dark heads of the Japanese tourists and my own. A woman waved at her, and Jane stepped over to chat. She accepted the cigarette that her coworker offered her, which surprised me, because I had not known that Jane smoked.

Then I saw Richard approach them. The day was warm, and he wiped his forehead with a handkerchief as he exchanged pleasantries with the coworker. It was strange to see Jane and Richard together outside of their house, or outside of a photograph in their house. Perhaps they had arranged to have lunch together that day. Then I remembered what day of the week it was. According to her schedule book, Jane spent every Tuesday afternoon at a doctor's on Park Avenue. When I had first peeked in the book, I had wondered over the two entries that had recurred the most: her lunch date with Evan and her standing doctor's appointment. Now I knew what the first one meant, but the second remained a mystery. In the short time that it took for Jane to put out her cigarette, take Richard's arm, and say good-bye to her coworker, I decided to abandon my lookout for Evan and follow Jane and Richard instead.

I lingered several paces behind them, keeping a number of people between us. When they stopped at a light, I scrutinized their appearances but neither seemed agitated or upset. They occasionally turned their heads toward each other in conversation, and Jane even smiled once at something Richard said.

When they got to Park Avenue they made a sharp turn into what looked like a residential building with its green awning and doorman and potted plants on either side of a wrought-iron gate. I stopped at the entrance to look at the list of names posted outside. Almost all were doctors. With rising alarm, I wondered if Jane had some illness she was keeping a secret from everyone. I thought she sometimes looked a little pale, but then she had a fair complexion. She didn't appear sick. Maybe she had one of those illnesses that couldn't be detected, that lurked beneath the skin. I immediately wondered if she died, what would happen to Lily? I couldn't imagine Richard taking care of her. Lily needed Jane; she needed a mother.

"May I help you?" the doorman asked.

"Dr. Silver?" I gulped.

"Fourth floor, Suite B."

I had no choice now but to go through the door under the doorman's watchful eye and step into the elevator. I got out on a floor that looked like that of a hotel, with a neutral-colored carpet and beige-striped walls and numbered doors extending on either side of the hall. I waited outside Dr. Silver's door until I figured enough time had passed so that Jane would have gone into her appointment. But what if Richard were out there waiting? Or would he have gone in to see Jane's doctor with her?

Curiosity got the better of me and I opened the door a crack. In that brief instant I saw that neither Jane nor Richard were there, so I slipped inside. The place I found myself in didn't look like where you would go if you were sick. The school clinic I had known back in China had a concrete floor and walls with the top half painted white and the bottom half painted mint green. Just a curtain had hung over the doorway, and the patients waited on a row of metal folding chairs outside in the hall.

This room looked like a living room, with comfortable chairs and tables with magazines strewn across them, plants in the corners, and a thin strain of music playing. Only one other patient was present, a large woman who hardly looked up from the crossword puzzle in her lap. Behind a glass window near the door was another woman who I guessed was a receptionist. She didn't seem to notice my entrance.

Quickly, I sat down in a chair across from the large woman. Her lips noiselessly sounded out the letters of a word.

"Excuse me," I whispered.

She looked up.

"Are you sick?"

The woman gave me a wry smile. "Honey, we're all sick in one way or another." She tapped the side of her head meaningfully.

I drew back from her, confused.

"Miss, do you have an appointment?" the receptionist called.

I retreated toward the door, suddenly realizing what the large woman meant. "Um . . . I'm sorry . . . wrong doctor."

~ ~ ~

From Western books and newspapers and movies, I knew what a therapist did, although I had never known anyone who had gone to see one. I had thought that only crazy people went to therapists. But I couldn't sense much that was wrong with Jane. There had been that one moment of sadness I had glimpsed when we had discussed Lily's birthday, but otherwise Jane seemed the capable, confident person I had always thought her to be. Then I remembered the time she and Richard had argued at dinner, and what Evan had said about Richard's character, about him not being much of a family man. The fact he had gone with Jane to her appointment implicated him in my eyes.

My impression of Richard was that he was a quiet man, often overwhelmed by Jane's and Lily's vivacity. His rumpled brown suits and partially shined oxfords in the closet didn't say much about him. Unlike Jane, he didn't leave his schedule book lying around. Often these days I didn't even see him. On weekdays he came home after Jane did, or, I was told, he stayed at work late and had dinner at the office.

One day, as I was finishing giving Lily her bath, I had heard the front door open and close, the thump of Richard's briefcase by the door, his heavy tread down the hallway. Lily struggled to be set free, but I wasn't about to let her run around the house naked. Jane was in the kitchen, and I supposed Richard had gone to meet her there.

Lily was squirming so much that it was impossible to dress her. I finally wrapped her up in a towel and carried her out of the bathroom. Maybe if she got to see Richard she'd calm down. Almost at the kitchen door I heard their raised voices: Jane's fragile like a glass on the edge of a table, Richard's low like an approaching storm.

"You've never been in this one hundred percent." *Jane.*

"I told you from the beginning that I didn't want this."

I couldn't see their faces but knew that Jane's cheeks would bloom red, as they did when she got worked up about anything. Richard would look calm beneath his beard, but his fingers would be clenched around dead air.

"That you didn't want her? Is that what you're saying?"

"That's not what I meant. *God,* you always—"

"What then? What is it you want?"

"I don't know."

Suddenly I noticed that Lily was very still in my arms. I held her closer, rested my head on her still-damp hair as if to shield her from what was going on.

"Well, all I know is that back then, something had to change. Either someone had to leave, or there had to be more than just the two of us."

"Then maybe that's where we are again."

Jane's voice was suddenly quiet. "Maybe so."

I had heard enough. I went back down the hall and into Lily's room, where I silently dressed her and she let me comb her hair without a fuss. Looking around the room at all the stuffed animals and dolls, the scallop-edged wallpaper and pastel-hued drawings, I wished we could stay in there forever.

Outside, people could shout and argue with each other, and here we would be safe.

After a while, there was a knock on the door. It opened to reveal Jane. The only thing that betrayed what had happened was the flush high in her cheeks.

"Oh, there you are," was all she said. In the way she averted her eyes from me when I left, I could tell that she still cared about appearances. But I wasn't sure for how much longer.

As I walked down the street away from the Templeton-Walkers' apartment that day, I noticed some things about the neighborhood for the first time. The hazy fall air could not mask how old the buildings were, the cracks in the brownstone facades, the paint flaking off the iron railings, the sidewalks stained with garbage. The lighted windows and the warm interiors they framed looked as unreachable as if they were on another planet. A young couple passed by me sharing in some private joke. I hated them for the way their scarves were draped over their shoulders, and for the sheer fact that they were laughing, as much as if they were laughing at me. Then I thought that once upon a time, Jane and Richard had been happy like that.

~   ~   ~

For the first time since I had started working for them, I was reluctant to go to their apartment. I was beginning to notice things about their home just as I had about the neighborhood—the buzzer that was always broken, the scratches that marred the wood-paneled floor, the water stains on the kitchen ceiling. Also, no matter what room I was in, the air felt heavy with unsaid words. If something was wrong with Jane and Richard's marriage, if something was going to happen to their family, I didn't want to learn about it through little clues and hints left behind at home.

The day before Lily's birthday party, I stayed when Jane returned from work so we could go over the final details. The party was being held on a Saturday, and I was to come early to help set up. It was assumed that I would stay the whole time to watch the other children, and afterward to help clean.

Jane had ordered a cake from a local bakery. It was to be in the shape of a dog, to make up for the fact that Lily was definitely *not* getting a dog for her birthday. There were toys in the front closet from friends and relatives, some which I had wrapped—more dolls, tea sets, books, videotapes. I had helped write and address invitations to six little boys and girls, their parents, and various friends of the family. Jane had come around to the idea of long-life noodles, and I was to pick those up, along with the red-dyed hard-boiled eggs and ginger, from Chinatown.

Now Jane and I sat at the kitchen table, sorting through the pile of RSVPs and assembling party-favor bags. Lily was in the other room obliviously watching television. She knew that a party was being held in her honor, and lots of people were going to be coming over, and she was going to be treated like a princess, but she had no idea how big of a deal it was to her parents.

I asked Jane what they had done for Lily's second birthday.

"We kept it very quiet," Jane said. "And her first birthday, of course, she had just come from China. Hardly any of my friends knew she had arrived. I was afraid for such a long time that I would jinx it if I told them. We had a welcome home party for her, but of course she wouldn't remember that."

The phrase "welcome home" struck me as odd. I thought about how nearly a year ago, I had first arrived in America. I still didn't think of it as my home. Only certain parts of it, like the park and the Templeton-Walkers' apartment, had ever remotely felt like that to me.

"In China," I said, "Lily would be four years old."

"How's that?"

"People think the time spent in the mother's belly counts. So when a child is born, she is already one year old."

"I like that idea. That a child is considered a person at the moment of conception. But I have to admit, I'm surprised to hear Chinese people think that." Jane gave me a sidelong glance. "Isn't abortion fairly common in China, with the One Child Policy and all?"

I was silent, my hands cold.

"By abortion, I mean getting rid of the child before it's born," she added gently.

I said, "If it were not for abortion, the One Child Policy would not work. And if the mother is unmarried, it will be hard for her to find a husband if she already has a child. If she is young, she will not be able to support it." I heard myself echoing my grandmother's views on the matter, and tried to still that voice in my head.

"I know, but it's such a backward way of thinking, that a woman can't have a child because of societal pressures. If she wants to have it, she should be able to have it. If she doesn't want to have it, she shouldn't have to. It should be that simple, but it isn't anywhere, not even in America. It's like in America women have to fight for legal abortion, and in China women have to fight for the right not to have one." Jane noticed that I had grown very quiet. "I'm sorry," she said. "I get kind of worked up about this issue. It's—well, it's very close to me."

"It happened to you?" I blurted out.

I was afraid I had offended her, but Jane just smoothed one hand over the other and placed them both on the table. "As a matter of fact, yes. I did have an abortion, many years ago."

An English phrase popped into my head, what people said when someone had died. I didn't know if it was appropriate, but I said it anyway: "I am sorry for your loss."

She gave me a weak smile. "There's nothing to be sorry about. I was young, and I had just moved to New York. There was this guy I met at a party one night. Even if we had known each other better, it would have been a bad decision."

"Do you—"

"Regret what I did? Every day. My head says I made the right choice, my heart says no. I thought all those years when I wanted to have children but couldn't was some kind of punishment. And then Lily"—she unconsciously turned her head in that direction—"was an angel. She was my second chance."

Second chance. I felt myself growing big with all the things I wanted to say. But Jane reached forward and touched my hand, startling me back into myself.

"I'm sorry for going on about it. I can't imagine what you think of me now."

"I think—" I said. "I think you are very lucky to have Lily."

"Yes. No matter what happens, I will always have her. To be honest, I don't know if I would have chosen adoption if I'd already had a child. I can't imagine life without Lily now. But sometimes I wonder what it would be like if she had an older brother or sister. And though she's real, she's here, I still think about what could have happened. I even talk about it sometimes, all the different scenarios. Not to everyone, of course. Richard, well, he would freak out at the thought of more children." She paused. "I know that he—that we—said some things to each other the last time you were here. I know you heard them. I want you to know that that won't happen again."

I nodded, with the awkward feeling of a child whose parents are promising her that they won't fight anymore.

"We're working hard on that, on saying how we feel without turning it into an accusation. And we're making progress, every week."

I thought of the doctor that Jane and Richard had visited. "With Dr. Silver?" I said.

Now I knew I had really crossed the line with Jane. Two red spots flared and subsided in her cheeks. "How do you know I go to see Dr. Silver?"

"I heard you mention his name on the phone . . . you had to change an appointment. . . ." I had never lied to Jane before.

She gave me a strange look. "Well, it's hardly a secret by now. I've been going to see Dr. Silver—who's a woman, by the way—for years, ever since I started living in New York. She helped me pull through so much: losing a child, wanting a child, having a child. . . . Now she's been helping Richard and me talk to each other."

"What is it like?" I asked.

"Therapy? That's right, I can't imagine therapy being much of a thriving field in China."

"It is for, how do you say, problems in other countries."

"Yes, it's for first-world problems. Well, therapy isn't that different from what we're doing here. Two people talking face-to-face. And you feel free to say anything, knowing that the other person will never tell anyone else what you've told them."

"But the person is a stranger?"

"At first, but after a while—in my case, years—your therapist becomes like your second family. That's probably not good doctor-patient relations, but I did feel, especially when I was younger, that Dr. Silver was like a mother to me. Without the judgment, of course. I could have never told my own mother that I had had an abortion. She's Catholic, for one thing. And our relationship had never been like that."

I thought of my relationship with my grandmother, how she had a way of finding out things that I never wanted her to know about. Her presence in my life had been that of a shadow behind a tree.

I suddenly became aware of the silence between myself and Jane. Then she said softly, "You know, you can tell me anything. . . ."

Lily came into the room and climbed into her mother's lap, a sulky look on her face that both of us knew well. "Mommy." She spoke with her eyes fixed on me, as if I were an extension of Jane. "I'm hungry."

Jane set her down on the chair between us. "Just a few more minutes, sweetheart. Hua and I are almost finished here."

Lily seemed to accept that and reached for one of the party-favor bags. I automatically moved it out of her reach and gave her one of the extra toys to play with as Jane and I finished up.

"So, for tomorrow," Jane said, looking through the RSVPs, "remember that Erin is allergic to peanuts, and Katerina is allergic to milk, and Sam can't have too much sugar or else he'll start 'bouncing off the walls,' as his mother has written here. . . ."

I tried to focus on what she was saying, but I was thinking about her earlier revelation. I now understood why Jane had wanted a child, why Lily was so precious to her. Were all children, in some way, a form of redemption for their parents? I thought of my own parents, whom I had barely known. Their lives while I was growing up had been filled with hard work and sacrifice. I doubted they had considered me in that light.

Beside me, Lily was busy dismantling the toy I had given her. She, for one, would be carrying a lot of weight on her shoulders when she grew up.

Chapter Twelve

All of the children at Lily's birthday party were bursting with sugar and excitement and the thrill of being away from their parents. Now I understood why parents hired strangers to take care of their children—if they didn't, they would go crazy. Everyone had gathered in the dining room for the cake cutting, but afterward the children tended to stay there or in the kitchen, while the living room seemed to have been designated the child-free zone. I could hear the adults' conversation drift down the hall now and then, talk of spas and stocks accompanied by the gentle clinking of glasses.

"Amy, put that down. . . . Sam, don't throw that. . . . Erin, come back here." I grabbed in vain at Erin Paulson (allergic to peanuts) as she ran out of the room.

At the doorway I looked back to make sure my six remaining charges would be okay without supervision. Lily, Amy, and Katerina (allergic to milk) were daubing cake frosting on the tablecloth as though it were finger paint. The two boys,

Sam (no sugar) and Abraham, were throwing grapes at each other. Two hours ago the room had looked festive with streamers and Chinese lanterns hanging from the ceiling. A remarkably detailed cake in the shape of a chocolate Labrador retriever had sat in the center of the table. Now the cake had been cut up and the floor was strewn with crushed goldfish-shaped crackers, cookie crumbs, and the remnants of a pin-the-tail-on-the-donkey game. At one end of the table were bowls with the long-life noodles, hard-boiled eggs, and gingerroot. None of the children had wanted to touch anything after Katerina had announced that the noodles looked like worms, so they had become just for decoration.

I hoped no one would get into trouble while I was gone and headed down the hall to look for Erin. She wasn't in the kitchen or the bathroom or either of the bedrooms, so there was only one other place she could be. I stood at the threshold of the living room, uncertain about entering. The adults at the party consisted of the mothers of the children, a few of the fathers, and some of Jane and Richard's child-free friends. They were standing in small groups, talking and eating off of regular china as opposed to the children's paper plates. Among the many heads, I spotted Erin's blond one. She leaned against her mother and stared at me as if daring me to drag her back into the kitchen.

"That's okay," Erin's mother said when she noticed me approach. "She can stay here." She turned and added to Jane, who was standing nearby, "You're so lucky to have a nanny who's willing to handle a birthday party."

"Yes," Jane said. "Hua's very helpful. So what were you saying about Erin's preschool?"

As I walked back down the hall toward the kitchen, the buzzer for the front door rang. I looked back but none of the adults seemed to have noticed. So I opened the door, expecting some late guest or maybe Richard, whom I had noticed leaving the apartment some minutes earlier. Evan and a young woman stood outside. I recognized her from the photo in his apartment. I was meanly glad to see that she was not as pretty and mysterious as her two-dimensional black-and-white self. Also, with her hair tied back in a ponytail, she looked younger and more innocent than I had expected.

"Hua, how are you," Evan said. He explained to the other woman, "Hua is Lily's nanny."

"Hi, I'm Julie." She moved to shake hands, but something in my face stopped her.

"Can we come in?" Evan asked.

I stepped back and let them through. The hallway was so narrow that they had to brush past me. A knee-jerk reaction of longing stirred in me at the faint smell of Evan's shaving lotion. Then it was eclipsed by a whiff of fragrance from Julie— not perfume but the more timid scent of soap—before it could get too far.

Other guests looked up as Evan and Julie entered the room, and I heard Jane's exclamation of welcome as she went to them. Julie offered her cheek to be kissed, once. She and Jane appeared to know each other, although I thought Jane's reaction to her was rather cool. I returned to the children, where in my absence Abraham had started to cry and Amy announced she was feeling sick from eating too much ice cream.

I was saved from dealing with these minor crises by Jane calling everyone into the other room to watch Lily open her presents. Lily loved all the attention. She sat in the big armchair looking like a princess with a paper crown sitting on top of her hair, which had been curled specially for the party. As the guests got into position, with the children in front of the armchair-throne and the adults behind them, Jane beckoned to me. She handed me a pad of paper and a pencil.

"For writing down the name of each child and their present," she whispered.

I nodded. Across from me, Evan took out a camera to capture the moment of each gift opening. Lily ripped through what wrapping paper and ribbons she could, and Jane helped her with the rest. Everyone marveled over the presents: an arts-and-crafts kit, a doll outfitted in historically accurate clothes from the eighteenth century, an interactive book that was supposed to teach your child how to read. The children seemed more impressed by the mounds of tissue paper and glitter and bows.

As the last gift was being opened, Jane looked toward the front door. Richard had snuck in with a huge, misshapen package tied with a bow. It was Lily's surprise present, kept in the storage room in the building's basement so she wouldn't see it. Now she tore away the paper to reveal a shiny red tricycle. The guests applauded, and I noticed that Jane and Richard gave each other a look of relief and satisfaction.

The party continued but I decided I would start cleaning up in the kitchen. On my way there, I heard a voice remark, "They're doing a good job pretending."

I stopped short and peered around the corner to see two women in the hallway, glasses in hand. I recognized one as Sam's mother, who before leaving Sam in my care had reminded me, loudly and slowly, not to let him eat too much sugar. I had immediately disliked her: her sharp features and frosted blond hair, the note of caution in her voice. She was speaking to another woman who looked far too loose-jointed and relaxed to be the mother of one of these children.

"They look fine to me," the childless woman replied.

"I'll just bet one of them is having an affair."

"You think so? Which one?"

"I don't know, maybe both of them. In any case, that's the look of a couple just before they split." Sam's mother drank from her glass. "I should know."

"Well, if they do split up, I feel sorry for Lily."

"But think of what she was saved from. She would probably have died of some third-world disease or grown up with no education or been sold into sexual slavery if she stayed in that place."

"Might be better than being a child of divorce. Less therapy later." Both of them laughed. Then, after a pause, the childless woman said, "Well, I think they look fine."

Sam's mother gave a snort. "It's an act. The happy family act. We all do it sometimes."

I didn't want to hear any more. Affairs, divorce, and therapy—these were the stuff of American families. I waited a moment, then hurried past the two women into the kitchen. They barely glanced at me.

As I stacked dishes in the sink, I remembered the look Jane and Richard had given each other after Lily had opened her present. Although they weren't standing close together, I knew that they must have felt the same thing: pride in their accomplishment of having raised such a beautiful child together. Those gossiping women had to be wrong. Jane and Richard and Lily were happy. No matter what words I had heard pass between them, they had to stay together for Lily's sake.

"Sorry to interrupt," a voice said. "I just wanted to get a glass of water."

I looked up to see Julie, Evan's ex-girlfriend—or whatever she was now—come in. She opened and closed cupboard doors as she looked for clean glasses. I didn't offer to help. She opened one door and said, "Wow. Look at all that cat food."

The cat came running from wherever it had been hiding since the guests arrived, and Julie knelt and spoke softly to it.

"I'm more of an animal person than a people person," Julie said as she scratched the underside of the cat's chin. "It was getting to be a little too much for me in the other room."

I nodded and pointed. "The glasses are over there."

"Thanks." Julie filled a glass from the tap and looked around the room. "This is an amazing apartment." Her eyes came to rest on me. "You're Lily's nanny, right?"

"Yes."

"Do you live here, too?"

"I live in Chinatown."

"What's that like? I mean, what's it like living there?"

I felt myself relax a little. "Noisy. Crowded."

I hoped she wouldn't ask me any more questions, or that she'd think I was a new immigrant and not worth talking to. But she set the glass down and leaned against the counter opposite me. "You speak English really well. Evan told me you had just come to the States."

My throat clenched at the thought of Evan discussing me with her, although I doubted he had told her everything. "Yes, but I learned English at school. You were born here?"

"In Queens. But my parents are from Taiwan."

"I know." I saw with satisfaction that she was starting to wonder what had been said about her, too.

"I wish I could speak Chinese. When I was little, my grandparents would visit. They didn't know any English, so I could never talk to them. Even now, on the phone, it's hard. My parents have to translate."

I thought of how strange and sad it would be if I couldn't communicate with my grandmother. "But you can learn?"

Julie made an impatient gesture. "I know, I know. I could have taken beginning Chinese in high school. But I took Spanish instead. I thought it would be more useful."

What could be more useful than learning the language that would allow you to speak to your own family members? I said, "You can learn now. It is not too late."

"Actually, it kind of is. I read somewhere that past the age of thirteen it's pretty hard to pick up a new language unless you have a special ability. Of course, some people take things too seriously. I overheard this mom in the other room talking about how many different languages she was exposing her child to, hoping one, in her words, 'would take.'"

I guessed that would be Katerina's mother. When they had arrived this morning, she had made Katerina say "happy birthday" to Lily in three different languages.

"Lily's lucky you're here to teach her Chinese."

It was true that I had managed to teach Lily a few words, those for 'mother' and 'father,' her name, and how to count to three. She treated it like a game. I sometimes spoke to her in Chinese and, perhaps it was my imagination, she seemed to understand some of it. Even though I knew Jane had some knowledge of Mandarin because of her work, I didn't think she—and definitely not Richard—spoke Chinese to Lily in my absence. If I weren't there, she wouldn't be getting any of her language at all.

"Evan knows some Chinese," I said. "He can teach you."

Julie made a face. "You're being too kind. Even *I* know his Chinese isn't that good. You must have heard him."

"Yes."

"And?"

"It is awful."

Julie laughed, and I was surprised to find myself joining in. "So what are they like to work for, Jane and Richard?"

I hesitated. "They are good people."

"Sure, but what are they *really* like? You must know all sorts of things about them." Julie raised an eyebrow. "Secrets."

I thought of the clothes in Jane's closet and her makeup that I had tried on, her red leather schedule book whose contents I had regarded as carefully as if they had come from her open heart. These weren't real secrets, not the kind that someone else would find titillating. But to me, these things I knew about Jane created a kind of tunnel through which I traveled to see what her life was really like. Then I thought of her and Richard's argument. The need to confide my fears in someone else loosened my tongue.

"I think they are having problems."

"With their marriage?" Julie's eyes widened, and I was reminded of Mrs. Ma at the boardinghouse when she was gossiping with a neighbor.

"I heard them fighting. I think Richard did not want Lily, before she came from China."

"Well, he probably wasn't as keen on adoption as Jane, but . . . I mean, Lily's here now. There's nothing he can do about it. He seems so devoted to her."

I struggled to speak my thoughts. "But he is not the father type."

"What do you mean?"

"Evan said—"

"Oh, Evan. He's just bitter about his own father. Did he tell you that, too?"

"Yes, his father was an artist."

"A famous artist. He probably didn't tell you that. And he probably didn't tell you that when his father died, he left most of his money to his second wife and new family. Can you imagine, walking around in some gallery and seeing your father's work, knowing that he thought so little of you at the end? Talk about family drama."

I had to admit that could make anyone bitter. "It happened long ago?"

"He was a teenager. At least his parents *got* divorced. Sometimes I think mine would have been better off if they had, but it would have been too shameful. You know how Chinese families are, divorce is still taboo. No one they know has gotten divorced, only their non-Chinese friends, and that's because they don't value family enough. Now, when I go home to visit my parents, it depresses me how far apart they've grown. It's like they can hardly stand being in the same room with each other."

I thought of Aunt May in her garden and Uncle George in the den. "Why?"

Julie shrugged. "They met when they had both just arrived in the States. There weren't many educated Chinese in the big cities then, and there was no question of marrying someone who wasn't Chinese. You had to take what you could get. For a long time I thought it was because they weren't capable of being in love, not in the way people in the movies are. But one day my mom showed me the photo she had of her college sweetheart back in Taiwan. She had saved it for forty years."

I thought of the wedding photo of my parents that my grandmother kept. Had my parents been in love then? You couldn't tell from their facial expressions, flattened by sepia and time. But if they had been, there wouldn't have been time for that love to fade. They never knew what it would be like to grow old together, but they also didn't know what it was like to wake up next to someone who had become a stranger. Maybe, in that way, they were blessed.

"Anyway," Julie said, "I don't think Jane and Richard are going to get divorced. Even if they did, I don't think Richard would abandon Lily. For one thing, Jane wouldn't let him."

"Did someone mention my name?" a voice called out.

Both Julie and I turned guiltily as Jane came into the kitchen.

"Hua's just been telling me about how nice it is to work for you and Richard," Julie said easily.

"That's good," Jane said. "Hua, can you go see to the kids in the living room? I'm afraid some of them are getting a little out of control." Without waiting to see if I had heard, she turned to Julie. Her smile seemed a trifle forced as she said, "I'm sorry I didn't get a chance to speak with you earlier. I'm so glad you and Evan could make it to the party. . . ."

While I picked up shredded paper and tattered ribbons from the floor, I thought about the way Jane had spoken to Julie. I didn't think I had imagined some kind of animosity between them, at least on Jane's part. Perhaps she had secretly been glad when Evan had broken up with Julie. And because she couldn't have him herself, she'd directed him to me instead. I was no threat to her; I depended on her for my job, for everything. She'd planned it—she'd wanted me to sleep with him. I was beginning to feel sick to my stomach.

Then I looked up to see Sam's mother frowning at me.

"Did you let Sam have a second piece of birthday cake?"

"Sorry?"

"Sam. You let him eat two pieces of cake."

I remembered now what had happened. Sam's mother had told me that he was allowed to have only one small piece of cake, but the moment she had gone into the other room, he had grabbed an extra slice and stuffed half of it into his mouth.

Obviously he had known this was off limits because he had swallowed it in two bites, giving me a chocolate-frosting grin in defiance. There was nothing, short of pinning him to the floor and sticking my hand down his throat, that I could have done about it. I wondered how Sam's mother knew. Then I saw that Sam was racing around the room, running into other people and knocking over glasses. I had an idea of what his mother had meant by "bouncing off the walls."

When Sam rushed by, his mother caught him by the arm and he started to howl. The other guests stopped talking and turned to stare as the wails rose higher and higher, crashing against the ceiling.

"See?" Sam's mother hissed at me. "This is what happens when he has too much sugar. You were supposed to look after him. I told you what to do."

My cheeks flushed with shame, then paled. I felt as if I were standing outside of myself, watching this strange standoff with the crying child between me and the angry woman. Vaguely I was aware of the people looking at us, recognized Richard's and Evan's faces. I opened my mouth, but I didn't get the chance to say anything.

"What's the trouble here?" Jane's voice inserted itself between us.

Sam's mother would not look at me. "Your nanny let Sam have another piece of cake, after I *explicitly* told her not to."

"Hua must not have understood you," Jane said. "She has trouble with English sometimes."

"Don't they all," Sam's mother said.

I stared at Jane, not believing what I had just heard. She returned my gaze, and something in it made me nod and look down. By now the wails had trailed off and Sam went limp in his mother's grip, exhausted from too much stimulation.

"Sugar crash," someone murmured.

The party dissolved soon after that. Jane and Richard, with Lily in Richard's arms, stood at the door to see their guests out. Evan and Julie were among the last to leave.

"I'll send you the pictures," I overhead Evan tell Jane.

Julie said good-bye to Jane and Richard, and then gave a little wave in my direction. I lifted my hand to return it, but she was already out the door. Evan noticed us and a puzzled look crossed his face, as if he was just beginning to grasp the idea that Julie and I might have talked about him behind his back. I smiled to myself at how much time he'd spend thinking about what we'd said. That was also when I realized I hadn't thought much about Evan myself for the past few weeks. It was possible to forget that kind of hurt.

After the last guest had left, Lily struggled to be put down and ran to her tricycle, but Richard took it away from her.

Jane said, "Not right now, sweetie, you'll ruin the floors if you keep on riding it in the house. We'll try it out in the park tomorrow." She looked at the untidy living room, the used dishes and glasses scattered about, the furniture all moved around, and sighed. "I'm exhausted."

"It's been a long day," Richard said.

Jane now seemed to notice me. "Hua, you can go home now."

"But . . ." I gestured to indicate the immensity of the task.

"We'll take care of it. You've done enough today." Jane walked me to the door. I stepped into the hallway, my feet reluctant, confused and hurt that she no longer wanted my help.

"Thank you for coming today," Jane said, then added, "I hope you didn't mind what I said to Sam's mother. About your English. She's just impossible to deal with. I had to come up with some excuse. I know it was an awful thing to say. So, see you Monday?"

The band around my heart loosened. "See you Monday."

Before I left, I looked back down the hall to where the Templeton-Walkers' living room was framed by the doorway. I couldn't see Lily, but Jane and Richard were sitting on the sofa with their backs to me, their heads inclined toward each other in what was possibly shared weariness, possibly something more. I walked down the street toward the subway, the doubt I had felt all day about Jane and Richard, and my place with them, lifted.

It was dark by the time I reached Chinatown, but the produce sellers were still on the street, their breath showing faintly white as they called out prices. In the hall of my building, Mrs. Ma was seeing out her own guests. She must have had some friends over for mah-jongg that afternoon.

"Hua, there's a letter for you on the table," she said.

I thanked her, took the letter, and went up the stairs to my room. It was an airmail letter with stamps from the People's Republic of China. My New York address was written in a shaky hand that looked as if it had copied the words without knowing what they meant.

I opened the letter and slid the single sheet of paper out carefully so it wouldn't tear. The Chinese characters leaped out at me in the dim light.

Dear Hua,

You will be surprised to be hearing from me. It is Old Luo, your neighbor who lived next door since you were a baby. I should also be writing to your relatives in America, but I do not know them and I feel you should know first. Perhaps you can tell them what I am about to tell you now.

Hua, I am very sorry, but about two months ago your grandmother became sick. It was something with her lungs. She tried herbs, acupuncture, even Western doctors. The money you sent was very useful for this. But she could not get better. A few days ago she went into the hospital. Hua, I am very sorry, but your grandmother has passed away. She went peacefully, and by the time you are reading this, her friends will have given her the funeral she deserved. So there is no use in you coming back home. I'm sure she would have wanted you to stay where you are and continue to work hard. She used the money you sent to pay off the remaining debt that brought you to America, so you don't need to worry about that.

I wish I had better news for you. But now your grandmother is with your grandfather, where she always wanted to be. So you should be glad for her, and continue to prosper in America.

Your friend,
Old Luo

Chapter Thirteen

The following days passed as though I were in a dream from which I desperately wanted to awake. The kind where you pinch or slap yourself, wake up, and then realize you're still dreaming. Then I began to think I had been living in a dream since I had come to America. The dream would end when I went back to China and saw my grandmother again, but now that would never happen.

Old Luo had mentioned money several times in his letter. Now I wondered if I had sent more money to my grandmother, maybe she would have been able to go to Shanghai to get better medical treatment. Or if my aunt and uncle in New Jersey had known about her illness, they might have been able to help out. I did not take Old Luo's suggestion and contact them. They would be sympathetic, but they couldn't change what had happened.

The only thing that kept me going was the routine of my days with Lily. I still took her to the park, sometimes with her new tricycle, although with the colder weather I had to bundle her up. Soon it would be too cold to take her outside. The winter stretched before me, the bleak streets of Chinatown with the slicing wind from the East River, brightened only by the prospect of the Templeton-Walkers' nonworking fireplace. By that time I had stopped wondering about the state of Jane and Richard's marriage, as if Jane and Richard themselves were frozen in the door frame in which I had last seen them together.

Then one Friday afternoon, about three weeks after Lily's birthday, Jane asked me to stay behind.

"You're the first to know this," she said, "but Richard and I are going to have a trial separation."

"What does this mean, trial separation?" I glanced at Lily, who looked too absorbed with a toy to be listening.

"Well, it means that Lily and I are going to stay here in this apartment, and Richard is going to find somewhere else to live in the city so he can work on his new play. It means that I am going to have to work full-time and put Lily in day care." She paused. "And, I'm afraid, it means that we're going to have to let you go."

"I don't understand."

"Hua, it's been great having you take care of Lily. But now she's old enough that I feel comfortable putting her in day care, and soon she can start preschool, and . . . well . . . it'll just be easier for all of us. I can write you a good reference if you want, ask around to see if anyone I know needs a nanny—"

"No!"

Jane looked taken aback by my vehemence. "Okay, then. Maybe your old boss will rehire you? You worked at a restaurant, right?"

To go back to the Lucky Duck would be a defeat. Only now did the full meaning of Jane's announcement become clear to me.

"When?" I asked.

"Next week, I'm afraid. That's the earliest I can put Lily in day care. I'll pay you for another week, though. I think that's only fair." Jane moved to touch my arm, but I shifted aside so that her hand fell in midair.

"I know this is upsetting," she said. "I'm pretty upset about it myself. Even though Richard and I have been talking about this for a while, it's hard to believe it's going to happen. And I don't know how it'll affect Lily. Richard will visit on weekends, of course, but she'll know something's wrong—"

"My grandmother died," I said. I don't know why I said it, but it came from the part of me that had been hollow for days.

For once, Jane appeared at a loss for words. Then she hugged me. "I'm sorry," she said. "You poor thing. I'm so sorry."

The familiar scent of her perfume surrounded us. I could tell from the staccato of her breathing that she was crying for me, for herself, and for Lily. This loss was something she thought she understood. But it had nothing to do with her, just as her and Richard's separation had nothing to do with me. It was only by chance that the circles of our lives had briefly overlapped.

It was hard afterward to act like nothing had happened. I said good-bye to Jane and Lily as I always did, and said that I would see them Monday morning. Lily looked from me to her mother, and I liked to think that she knew something was going on. I wondered what Jane would tell her when I failed to appear one day. The thought that Lily would forget me made my heart shrink into itself.

I left the apartment and headed for the subway. While waiting for the train, I heard a sound that hadn't touched my ears
since leaving China. It was the voice of an *erhu,* the two-stringed
instrument with a belly as round as a cooking pot and a neck
straight like a crane. It was a song I didn't know, the Western
notes bending so that they glided dark and cool through the air.
I followed the sound around a pillar and saw Li, one of the cooks
from the Lucky Duck.

"What are you doing here?" I exclaimed.

"Hua?" Li seemed just as surprised to see me. "What are
you doing here?"

"I work near here." I remembered what had happened to
me that day. "I used to work near here. Oh, never mind. How
is the restaurant?"

"Didn't you hear?"

I shook my head. Mrs. Ma hadn't talked about the Chous
for weeks.

"Old Chou gambled the restaurant away! The new owner
turned it into a massage parlor. He offered Xiao Ru a job but
she left to work in a restaurant down the street. He didn't want
the rest of us, of course. Gao doesn't have a new job yet. He
wants to find a partner to open a dumpling stand with him."

A wry smile crossed my face at the thought of Gao trying
to convince someone to go into business with him. "And you?"

Li shrugged. "I don't want to work in a restaurant anymore.
It's too dangerous." Unconsciously he favored the hand that
he had injured months ago. "So I'm trying to make some
money this way." He held up the *erhu.*

"Why don't you play your guitar?"

"Too many people play the guitar in these subway tunnels.
If I play the *erhu,* I'm different. And, you know, it's what the
tourists expect. Shall I play something for you?"

I tried to think of my grandmother's favorite song, any song from back home, but my mind was blank. "Play something you like."

"Okay." Li poised the bow above the strings.

It was a song that I slowly began to recognize. I had heard it before at school, played not on an *erhu* but on a piano. The words had been sung by a choir. It was a Western song, a hymn called "Amazing Grace." I had always thought it was about a woman named Grace who did extraordinary things, finding people who were lost, making them whole again. The sweet, mournful notes resonated in the subway tunnel.

~ ~ ~

There was no one to save my parents from the fire that took their lives. They couldn't even save each other. Their deaths could be blamed on factory negligence, the fact that there were no laws that limited the amount of workers in a room with only one exit. But my grandmother blamed history most of all for not allowing my parents a decent education, so that they ended up qualified only for unskilled jobs. As I was growing up, she was fiercely protective of me, making sure that I got into the girls' school, encouraging my friendship with Swallow and her influential family, and later, when these things did not work out, arranging for me to come to the States. But there were some things she could not protect me from.

After what had happened between me and Teacher Zhang, I lost all interest in school. My grades in his class suffered, as they did in my other subjects. I never raised my hand anymore to answer questions, afraid of being singled out by the teachers. When I walked down the halls, I felt that my classmates could tell that something was wrong with me, that I deserved to be shunned. Also, I was skipping classes because I was starting to feel sick. It was easier to just sit by the river and let the cool breeze soothe my nausea.

Naturally, being reluctant to teach us about sexual intercourse, our teachers had also told us nothing about pregnancy. But I had read enough to suspect what was going on with my body. I felt like I had swallowed a stone, and now it was sitting heavy and irretrievable at the bottom of my stomach. I worried that my classmates or teachers might suspect something, but it was almost Spring Festival. School would be out for almost two months, and I could hide my secret at home.

By then Teacher Zhang had left the school. Rumor had it that he had returned to Shanghai, but I never thought that I might track him down to tell him I was pregnant. I didn't even entertain the fantasy, as I supposed some girls in my situation might, that he would declare his love for me and marry me and take me to the big city. Ever since he had stopped acknowledging my presence, I had tried not to think about him in that way. I knew how important his job and reputation were to him. Sometimes I thought he would rather call me a liar than admit doing anything wrong. In my heart I knew he couldn't be that cruel, but at the time I thought so badly of my own behavior that my despair extended to everyone else.

My grandmother knew within the first week I was home. She said she could tell by the color of my cheeks, the way I walked as if I were balancing something precious on the top of my head. She said that was how she knew my mother had been pregnant with me. I suppose she could also have guessed something was wrong by how I stayed in bed for days. She reacted with remarkable quickness and efficiency, and scheduled me an appointment to get rid of the baby. She didn't trust the local hospital and didn't want to chance running into someone we knew, so she found a clinic in Shanghai. This was the only choice I had.

Once, I tried to question the decision my grandmother had made for me. But I got no further than, "What if—"

"Don't be a silly girl," my grandmother said. "Are you thinking you could raise a baby, even with my help? I had a hard enough time raising you. Besides, you need to finish school and get a job. You can't do that with a youngster hanging on to you. And you'll never find a husband who wants to take on a child that isn't his." She softened her tone. "Don't be afraid. Your mother had this procedure done, too."

I was surprised she would reveal this about my mother, whom she rarely talked about.

"When?"

"You were only two years old at the time."

"Didn't she want to have another child?"

My grandmother didn't have to answer. I could guess that my parents were too poor to bribe the local officials to turn a blind eye and let them have a second child. I wondered if my mother had agonized over her decision, or if she had thought of hiding in the countryside until the child could be brought to term, as many women did. Or maybe she had listened to the advice of her mother, my grandmother, without a word of protest, as I appeared to be doing.

Inside, I didn't know what to do. The more walks I took by the river, the more tempted I was to throw myself into its depths. When I saw a bus pass by me, bound for another town or province, I wanted to jump on and escape to a place where I could start another life. Most of all, I didn't want to let go yet of the baby growing inside of me. But the longer I waited, the more difficult it would be. I had heard reports of babies being killed upon leaving the mother's body, before they could utter their first cries. I knew I would never be able to recover from that.

My grandmother tried to make our trip to Shanghai as pleasant as possible, almost as if we were going on vacation. She got us soft-seat sleeper train tickets so that we could sit in our own compartment rather than in the hard-seat section crowded with smokers and crying children. When we got to the city, we stayed overnight in a cheap but clean guesthouse and spent the morning sightseeing. We ate French croissants and Shanghai soup dumplings, and went shopping in the fashion district that used to be part of the French concession. Only once did I think about how I might be walking down the same streets Teacher Zhang had when he was growing up.

I had never been to a city as big as Shanghai. It felt like two cities at once, with the ornate nineteenth-century buildings of the Bund on one side of the Pearl River and modern skyscrapers on the other. Although I had seen the occasional Westerner in Fuzhou, foreign tourists and students and businessmen crowded the streets here. The locals looked prosperous, too, more similar to the well-dressed foreigners than the people back home. My grandmother and I were in the middle, obviously provincial but better off than the peasants who had come in from the countryside looking for work.

At one point our walk took us into the older part of the city south of the Bund, away from the tall, modern buildings. It was a maze of tin-roofed, brick-walled houses that would have fit into the poorer parts of Fuzhou. Occasionally, at an intersection of the narrow lanes, produce and meat were laid out in an impromptu market. My grandmother looked over the vegetables, poking them with her finger to test for freshness. Once I looked up and saw a barefoot child staring at me from across the street. Its face was so dirty and its clothes so plain that I couldn't even tell if it was a boy or a girl. But I felt as if the child's eyes pierced through me, right into my belly, to what was growing inside.

My grandmother noticed me looking at the child and took my hand. "Come," she said. "We can't miss your appointment."

At the clinic, a female doctor told me what the procedure would entail. "Do you have any questions?" she said at the end.

"Does this happen often?" I whispered.

The doctor's mouth was set in a thin line. "It used to be mostly married women sent by the heads of their housing units. Now we're seeing more and more unmarried women with this problem. It's especially bad in the summer with the high school and college girls."

"What can you do about these girls?" my grandmother said with a weak shrug. "Too many Western movies, too much pop music."

I knew she was trying to find some way to explain the mistake I had made, not only to the doctor but to herself. How could I have done such a shameful thing? Was it because I hadn't had parents to properly bring me up? Was it something she had failed to teach me? Or was I just an ignorant, disobedient girl? I didn't know myself.

On the train ride home, my grandmother finally asked who the man was that had gotten me into this situation. I told her the truth.

"I have to tell the school," she said.

"But he'll lose his job."

"Why do you want to protect a man who took unfair advantage of you, one of his students?"

"I don't want anyone else to know." I didn't want to be the cause of Teacher Zhang's undoing, even if he had been the cause of mine.

"Do you think I want everyone to know? I'm sure the school will be discreet. They can't afford the risk of the parents knowing and thinking their daughters aren't safe. But they must know that this man has shamed you."

Somehow, the rumors got out. When I returned to school, teachers and classmates alike whispered about me, distorting the story until I began to doubt the part I had played in it. I couldn't concentrate in class and my grades slipped further. I think the principal was glad when she informed me I would not be able to graduate at the end of the year. That way I would fall silently from the record books, the girl who had seduced a teacher and ruined his reputation.

The summer after that was unbearable. While my classmates were looking for jobs, I stayed at home with my grandmother and helped her sew. She figured I could at least learn to do something useful with my hands. Sometimes I couldn't stand to be inside and took long walks to the edge of our neighborhood where the farmland began. During those times I would think about what it would be like if I were still pregnant. How big my stomach would be, whether I would be able to feel the baby stirring inside.

Seeing my listlessness, my grandmother began planning to send me to America. Without my knowledge, she made arrangements with my aunt and uncle in New Jersey and the necessary people in town that would arrange for my passage. I was more relieved than excited when she finally told me what she hoped for me. Rather than a bus, it was a plane that would take me out of this city and on to another life.

A year later, this new life I thought I had created for myself was over. It had vanished the moment Jane told me she no longer wanted me to work for her. I told myself that life for the Templeton-Walkers was going to change, too. Lily would be in day care and see her parents less, with her father away and her mother working all the time. But she and Jane would still have each other. I didn't fit into their equation; the two of them didn't need me in the way I needed them. They didn't even need Richard.

Furthermore, once I left, there would be no reason for me to come back. At first Jane might invite me over once or twice, but eventually she would forget about me and she and Lily would disappear from my life, just as everyone else who had been important to me had. I would never be able to see Lily grow older, learn how to tie her shoes, or read her first book. I would never see her again.

~ ~ ~

When I arrived at the apartment on my last day, Jane had finished giving Lily her lunch and was about to leave for the museum.

"I left you an envelope on the kitchen table," she said. "We'll talk when I get back." She glanced at Lily, a line appearing between her brows, and I realized that she hadn't told Lily yet. It was as if she was leaving the decision up to me—what to say and when to say it. I wondered how she and Richard had told Lily that Richard was leaving.

"Have a good time, girls." Jane kissed Lily good-bye, waved a hand at me, and hurried out the door.

On the table I found the envelope stuffed with bills: my payment for the next week. If this made Jane feel better for getting rid of me so abruptly, that was fine with me. I could use the money where I was going.

I walked through the rooms of the apartment. A few things had changed since Jane had made her announcement. I noticed that some of Richard's suits and pairs of shoes were missing from the closet, while Jane's clothes were spread out to fill the extra space. The cream-colored coat Jane had worn when I had first seen her had been moved toward the front in preparation for winter.

Standing in the living room, I remembered how the room had looked during Lily's birthday party. Today the black cat was sitting on the armchair that had been the seat of honor. About a week after the party, Jane had shown me the photos Evan had taken and sent her. I had nodded and smiled while she clicked through the pictures on the computer but had thought how easily the camera could lie. There were pictures of Jane and Lily, Richard holding Lily, even one of Jane and Richard standing side by side with their hands not quite touching. And then there was a picture of Lily and Jane and Richard together, after Lily had unwrapped her tricycle, surrounded by mounds of shiny paper. They looked like the happiest family in the world.

Purely by accident, I was in one of the pictures, too. I was in the background, my face turned away from the colorful tangle of children playing with discarded ribbons. Looking at the blurred version of myself, I knew I would always be apart from what was going on, no matter what room I was in. It was as if I lived in another place that had nothing to do with the reality of parks and brownstones and art museums. And I was convinced now, with Jane and Richard's separation, that Lily belonged there with me. Perhaps she would feel the lack of two parents, as I sometimes had, but I had my grandmother's example to follow. I hadn't realized until her death how much of a family the two of us had been. As Lily and I could be.

I took Lily into her room and changed her into warmer clothes. The pink coat from last winter was too small for her now, but her parents had bought her a beautiful new red one. I debated whether to take her favorite book or her favorite toy, which as of last week was a stuffed elephant. She loved having the book read to her, but she held the elephant when she went to sleep. I decided on both.

In the street, I hailed a taxi. It had been hard enough getting to Chinatown on the subway last time, and now I didn't have the stroller because it would be too much for me to carry. I gave the cabdriver the address and sat back, holding Lily on my lap. She turned her head to look at the park as we passed by it, but she didn't seem disturbed by this change in plans.

"Don't worry, Lily," I told her. "We're going on another adventure."

When we got to the boardinghouse in Chinatown, I asked the driver to wait and watch Lily while I went upstairs to get my things. At the front door I looked back, suddenly fearful that he would drive off with her, but he only turned up the radio.

In my room, I grabbed the bag I had packed the night before. It was very light, considering it held all the memorable things from my past year in New York: the letters I had received, a couple of books, the white pebble from the Templeton-Walkers' apartment, Evan's penknife. But the most important thing I was taking was downstairs in the taxi, waiting for me.

As I approached the front door, I heard a door open behind me in the hall.

"Hua." I heard Mrs. Ma's voice. "Do you have a moment?"

I supposed she had some kind of complaint. Well, it didn't matter; I wasn't going to be around much longer. I checked to make sure the cab was still outside, dropped my bag by the door, and stepped into her apartment.

The place was funereal with curtains that had been drawn against the light. Perhaps the mysterious Mr. Ma had passed away, although I suspected he had been out of the picture for a long time. It couldn't be Mrs. Ma's daughter because she had gotten married only a few weeks ago. I had seen the red paper characters posted outside the front door celebrating the event. In the middle of the gloom, Mrs. Ma sat on a sofa that was still encased in plastic. Then I noticed the bottle of *baijiu* and cup on the coffee table.

"Is everything all right?" I asked.

Mrs. Ma blinked and swallowed. "My daughter is going to leave me."

I tried not to laugh at her solemn tone of voice. "Where is she going?"

"She and her husband are moving to Maryland, to be closer to his family. What about me? I asked her. I'm all alone here."

"She can still call you," I said.

"But what if something happens to me? Right now she can get across town in half an hour. After she moves, it'll be half a day." Mrs. Ma poured herself another cup of *baijiu*.

"I have to go now," I told her, gently.

Mrs. Ma nodded as if she expected everyone to leave her. "Let me tell you, Hua, what they say back home is true. It's useless to have a daughter. They just leave you for another family."

In the taxi, Lily looked just as I'd left her, her stuffed elephant in one hand and the thumb of the other stuck in her mouth. She looked forlorn and a little scared. But when she saw me, she smiled, and I knew I had made the right decision.

"Where to now?" the driver asked.

"The Port Authority bus terminal," I said.

Part V

Chapter Fourteen

"Salina!" The bus driver called out the name of the next stop.

I stretched, clearing my head of sleep. I looked out the dark window at the fields that bled into each other. It was nearly midnight on the second day of our trip, and I had no idea where we were. Lily napped with her head on my shoulder, breathing warm puffs of air against my arm. I wondered what she was dreaming about. Was she thinking about New York? Would she awaken, frightened that she wasn't in her own bed?

Back in New York, Jane and Richard would be living a nightmare. It would have taken a while for them to realize what had happened. Jane would have returned from work and been puzzled that Lily and I weren't there to greet her, but she would have assumed we were at the park. She'd kick off her shoes and pour herself a glass of wine and start planning what to do for dinner. In half an hour she'd become impatient and, more than a little bit annoyed with me, throw on a coat and go to the park to find us, a reproach on the tip of her tongue. That annoyance would change to fear once she saw that we weren't there. The park would be almost empty, the leafless trees casting shadows in the twilight.

She'd call Richard, who would still be at work, and for the first time in days he'd come home. They'd contact the local hospitals and the police, asking whether they knew of anything that had happened to a three-year-old Chinese girl, possibly accompanied by her nanny, also Chinese.

Next, Jane would call the number I had left her, which belonged to the phone in the hall of Mrs. Ma's boardinghouse. It would ring many times before Mrs. Ma roused herself from her *baijiu* stupor and slapped down the hall in her cloth slippers to answer. Yes, she had seen me that day, I had been on my way out . . . no, she didn't know if I had returned. Could she go and check, please? It was very important. Well . . . Mrs. Ma supposed she could. My room wouldn't look much different than it usually did, and Mrs. Ma wouldn't notice anything missing. *Hua isn't here,* she'd say curtly and start to hang up, but Jane would keep her on the line. *Please,* she'd say, *do you have any children?*

Mrs. Ma would reply, cautiously, that she had a daughter.
Then you must understand what it's like.

Eventually Mrs. Ma would give Jane the number of the Chous. Old Chou would be home, his wife having banished him there after he'd gambled away their restaurant. This was the only way she could make sure he wouldn't be at Off-Track Betting or a basement card game. With nothing to do, he'd be playing solitaire and watching his wife's videotapes of her favorite Taiwanese soap operas. He hadn't seen me in weeks. Did he know how to get in touch with my relatives in New Jersey? He did not. Jane told him the police were involved, and that anything he knew would be helpful. But any mention of the police would make Old Chou forget his already shaky English.

Now the police would suggest to Jane, gently, that maybe Lily and I had been separated. Maybe they should concentrate on finding Lily first. Did they think I could have let someone take her from the park?

No, Jane would say. *She loves Lily. She'd protect her with her own life.*

Do you think your nanny could have taken your daughter somewhere herself?

What do you mean?

Has your nanny been behaving normally? Has she been upset about something?

Jane would recall our last interaction. *Her grandmother died recently. She was sad about that. And I told her we were putting Lily in day care so we wouldn't need her to babysit anymore. But . . .*

Mrs. Walker—

Ms. Templeton, please.

—do you think that your nanny might have taken Lily?

At first, Jane would refuse to consider that possibility. I had always been polite and respectful. I had never taken anything from their apartment, as far as she knew. I had been treated like a member of the family, so there couldn't be any reason I would resent or hate them. She couldn't think of me as a criminal; it went against everything she believed in. But gradually, with the urging of the police, she'd admit that it was the most likely scenario. And maybe Jane would realize, with a sense of foreboding, how much of a stranger I really was to her. She had never seen where I lived, never met my landlady or former employer or relatives. The stories I had told her about my grandmother and life in Fuzhou could have been made up. She couldn't be sure about anything.

We should try to track down her relatives in New Jersey, Richard would say. *What's their last name?*

Wu, I think, Jane would reply.

Lady, the policeman would say. *Do you know how many Wus there are in the phone book?*

That night Jane would walk through the rooms, picking up stuffed animals, building blocks, parts of a plastic tea set. She would put the toys away in Lily's room; she'd want everything to look the same when her daughter came back. She would be reminded of how she had prepared the room for Lily's arrival over two years before, when a baby was little more than a promise. That quickly, two years had been snatched away from her.

In the other room, Richard would hear Jane moving about in the home that he was no longer a part of. It would be the first time in a week or more that he would spend a night there. In the early morning hours he would convince Jane that both of them needed some rest. They would lie down on the bed and sleep without being disturbed until the sun reached the top corner of the window. They would wake in a loose embrace, having unconsciously moved toward each other in the dark.

~ ~ ~

I had thought of my aunt and uncle when the bus was leaving New York and entering New Jersey, en route to Pennsylvania. Just a turn at the end of the tunnel and we could change our destination. I could confess to what I had done, and my aunt and uncle would take Lily back for me. I could stay in their house, sleep in my cousin's bedroom, garden with Aunt

May, watch television with Uncle George. It was the last chance I had to back out of the path I had chosen, which was beginning to stretch before me farther than the horizon.

But I didn't look back, and with each city that passed my resolve grew stronger. Milesburg and DuBois in Pennsylvania; Cleveland, Ohio; Elkhart and South Bend, Indiana—I had never heard of these places. They were part of an America I hadn't known existed. They were similar to each other, with their indistinguishable bus stations. The windows reflected towns and sprawling farms, fields of grain that had not been harvested. The only thing that held my attention was the sky, curved overhead like an inverted blue porcelain bowl. It was larger than anything I could have imagined.

Once, I thought about how Jane had come from this part of the country with its uniform landscape. I wondered what it would be like growing up in one of the small towns we passed through, where the main street was punctuated by a church. I could see how someone would dream of escaping to a large city, of being hemmed in by buildings instead of open space. I thought of lifting Lily to the window and pointing out that this was where her mother had come from. Except I didn't want to remind Lily of her old life.

That first day Lily had been full of questions: Where were we going? When would we get there? How long before we stopped again? Then the questions became more insistent: Where was Mommy? When were we going back home? Where was Mommy? She wanted Jane. She asked for Richard, too, but less frequently. Afraid that other passengers would notice and wonder about the little girl who kept asking for her mother, I would say to her, "Mommy will meet us when we get there. You'll see her soon."

The lying bothered me. I had heard somewhere that memory begins at the age of three. Certainly I didn't have many memories of my parents. But even if Lily might not remember Jane, she might remember being lied to. She might remember the feeling of waiting for someone who never came, and I would be the one who had disappointed her. Hearing her ask repeatedly for Jane in her small, plaintive voice, I knew I would never hear her speak to me in the same way. Lily had learned to call a strange woman mother once; I wasn't sure if she would be able to do it again. I thought of the diary where my cousin had written that she hated her parents. Maybe it would be a good thing that Lily wouldn't call me mother, if American children ended up hating the people who'd brought them up.

~ ~ ~

The next morning, as Jane and Richard were waking to another day of uncertainty, Lily and I were in Chicago changing buses. This place felt more familiar, with its wide, gray, dirty spaces filled with the echoes of faulty brakes and garbled announcements.

As Lily and I sat in a corner of the station, I decided that we couldn't carry so many things. Reluctantly, I set aside her stuffed elephant and picture book. New toys could be bought when we arrived. Clothes, too, could be replaced, and it was warm where we were going so we wouldn't need much. It would be better to get rid of everything we had brought with us, so we had no reminders of the past. All we needed were the clothes on our backs. I tossed out more, creating a half circle of discarded items.

A shadow passed over our heads. I looked up to see a man with long gray hair and a grizzled beard. The smell of alcohol overpowered any other odors that might have come from his clothes, which looked like they hadn't been washed in months. His right pants leg was rolled up to reveal—nothing. The man was missing a leg.

He labored to speak, blowing out as much whiskey breath as words: "You people." He pointed unsteadily with one crutch at the belongings scattered around us. "You boat people. The government's brought you all the way over from Saigon. Gave you a house and job. I want to know, what'll the government do for me? I been waiting thirty years. What for?"

I didn't know what to say.

Giving a little hop on his good leg, he raised his voice. "I served my country. Lost more than what you see missing. What for, you tell me?"

He shook the crutch in my direction.

"You tell me!"

"I don't know!" I shouted back, more out of fear than defiance.

The man shifted on his foot and held out a paper cup. "You got a quarter then?"

I hesitated and thought of the meager bills in the small cloth purse I kept hidden underneath my shirt, the way my grandmother had taught me to carry valuables. I had used most of my salary from Jane to pay for bus tickets. "I don't have any change."

"I'll take a dollar then."

Meekly, I fished out a crumpled bill and put it in his cup. "Thank you."

He bowed and stumped off.

An elderly woman with blue-tinted hair had paused to watch our interaction. Now she leaned close enough so that I got a whiff of her old-lady smell, a combination of ancient lipstick and perfume.

"Don't feel bad, dear," she said. "You know he wasn't talking about you, don't you?" She patted me on the shoulder and walked away, her suitcase rolling behind her like a dog on a leash.

I nodded too late, looking from her to the back of the man limping his way across the station. I couldn't tell who was worse, the crazy veteran or the condescending old lady.

The bus was more crowded leaving Chicago than when we had arrived. I put Lily on my lap to make room for a girl who wore baggy clothes and grimy sneakers, an outfit I supposed was favored by teenagers everywhere across the country. She had sandy hair and freckles, and she looked around the bus in a way that made me think she was hungry, although not for food. She settled in her seat without looking at me or Lily.

I must have drifted off because I awoke with the distinct feeling that someone was watching me. The girl was staring at us with blue eyes paler than water. When she noticed I was awake, the corners of her mouth turned up slightly.

"Cute kid you got there."

I nodded. The girl's voice was hoarse and knowing, although she didn't look much older than a kid herself.

"Where you two from?"

"New York. And you?" I added politely.

"A little town, you wouldn't have heard of it." A pause. "Where you going?"

I hesitated, then answered, "California." For a long time this destination had only been a thought in my head. On the road, watching the fields pass by, it had seemed as hard to reach as if it were across an ocean. But finally saying it out loud made me think it was possible. "We are going to Los Angeles."

"Oh yeah? Me, too. You want to be an actress or something?"
I stared at her blankly.

"You know, Hollywood?"

"No, we are going to visit friends." I thought of Ah Jing's
letter folded up in my pocket; its closeness lent me strength.
Her new house bloomed in my mind, bright and safe. I'd take
Lily to the beach, hold her hand as she stepped in the water
with her bare feet. Her skin would grow tan and freckled, and
soon she'd forget what the cold felt like.

"We got a long ride ahead of us," the girl said. "But the bus
is luxury to me. Most of the time I hitchhike."

"What is that?"

She stared at me in disbelief. "You never heard of hitch-
hiking? It's like, you stand by the side of the road or at a gas
station and stick out your thumb and a car stops for you. Cheap-
est way to get around."

"Is it dangerous?"

"Can be. You gotta know who to trust. I never get in a car
unless it's a couple or an old lady or something. There are plenty
of men out there who'd take advantage of a girl like you or me."

I was surprised that this girl thought we were anything alike.
We were both going across the country, but I had a responsibility. There was no way I could hitchhike with a child. There
was something about this girl that I didn't want to be associ-
ated with: her odd eyes, or the half mumbling way she talked.
Then I thought of a way to get past her toughness.

"Do your parents know where you are?"

Startled, she laughed. "You think I ran away from home?"

"Do they?"

"No," she admitted. "I left home without telling anyone.
Probably didn't notice I was missing until the next day, and

even then they wouldn't care. Didn't care for years, don't see why they'd start now."

In the petulance of her voice I could finally tell how young she was. I felt sorry for her. She was wrong about her parents not caring, in thinking that by running away she was punishing them more than she was punishing herself.

I wanted to tell her this, but she turned away from me, leaned back in her seat, and closed her eyes. She didn't open them for the next few towns that we passed through. It was as though she wouldn't notice if someone tried to steal the sneakers off her feet. Her bluish, almost transparent eyelids reminded me of a baby bird whose eyes haven't opened yet.

Somewhere, this girl had parents that were worried about her. They must have suspected that she had run away from home. But that was little comfort, to know that your child might be safe but unwilling to return to you.

~ ~ ~

"Salina! Ten minutes until the next bus leaves!"

I roused Lily. She would need to use the bathroom, and I would need to get us something to eat. Then I reached for my bag and found it was gone. It wasn't anywhere under the seats or nearby. I noticed the seat next to me was empty, too. Had the runaway girl taken my bag? She couldn't have known it had only a few things, the souvenirs from my time in New York. I patted my shirt to make sure my cloth purse was still there. At least she didn't get any money.

Then I realized our tickets, which would allow us to transfer to the next bus, had been in my bag. The girl wouldn't have to hitchhike to Los Angeles; she could take the bus all the way there. If that was even where she had planned to go.

We were being hustled off the bus. I sat Lily down on a bench in the station, trying not to show how worried I was. "Stay here," I told her and went to the ticket window. I tried to explain to the man behind the counter what had happened.

"Sorry, miss." He pointed to a sign on the wall that said the bus company was not responsible for lost, destroyed, or stolen tickets.

"But someone took my bag."

"All thefts should be reported to the police. Want me to call them?"

I tried not to reveal how much that thought alarmed me. "No, thank you," I said to him. "We are fine."

I went back to the bench and sat next to Lily, holding her hand. She was all I had left. It was midnight now, and the bus was due to leave. I watched as it pulled out of the station, taking my hopes for California with it.

Chapter Fifteen

Jane would have been horrified if she had seen how Lily and I had spent that night in the bus station. For dinner, we had potato chips and sodas from the vending machine. Fortunately, Lily thought it was great fun to push the buttons and choose from the colored packages. I told her we were camping, and she slept across two seats with her head pillowed in my lap and my old black coat draped over her. I drowsed against the concrete wall, but every time someone walked by my head would jerk up. The bus station was kept open twenty-four hours, and late-night buses passed through.

Also, I kept thinking of ways I could make enough money to buy new tickets. I could beg, like the Vietnam vet in the Chicago station, but that would take forever. We couldn't hitchhike; that wouldn't be safe, although staying in the Salina bus station seemed hardly safer. I needed to find a way to turn the few dollars I had on me into more than a hundred.

In the early morning, when there was no one else around, I left Lily to get up and stretch. I walked past the ticket counter, its shade drawn down, to the bus schedule posted on a wall. Another bus to Los Angeles would be coming by that night, and the night after that, but there was no way Lily and I could get on it.

Then, next to the bus schedule I saw a sign that said SHUTTLE TO RACETRACK, followed by a list of times. I had never been to a racetrack, but supposed it must have the tense atmosphere of one of Mrs. Ma's mah-jongg games, multiplied tenfold. Immediately I thought of Old Chou and how he had lost his restaurant through gambling, the Off-Track Betting in Chinatown with its cluster of desperate men. I was now more desperate than any of them.

Briskly, I woke Lily up. "We're going to see some horsies today," I told her. "Don't you want to see the horsies?"

She nodded, grumpily. I took her to the public bathroom to wash up, and I let her choose Oreos from the vending machine for breakfast. In another hour we were on the bus to the racetrack in a neighboring town, along with some old men who spent the whole trip with their eyes on their racing forms.

As we entered the racetrack grounds, Lily began to bounce up and down in her seat with excitement. I supposed she thought we were going to the circus or a fair or an amusement park. I had to admit that the place appeared festive. The stands looked like they stretched almost to the sky, and state flags fluttered in the breeze. The sun shone down on the gleaming green infield and the horses' glossy coats. It seemed like a lucky day.

I spent a few more precious dollars on a program and some popcorn to keep Lily quiet while we waited for the first race to start. I wasn't ready to bet until I could figure out what was going on. But the names and numbers in the program made no sense to me, and I couldn't tell which horse was which as they flew around the track. As the pack of horses passed in front of the stands, a roar rose from the crowd, and Lily and I shrieked, too. I looked around and saw men's red faces, eyes bulging. I thought I could even spot a few Old Chous among them.

For the next race, I took Lily down by the rail so we could watch the horses parade by.

"Pretty horsies!" Lily announced.

"Which one is the prettiest?" I asked.

"That one." She pointed to a chestnut horse whose jockey wore pink and blue silks. I supposed this method of picking a horse was as good as any. I put down two dollars and it came in third, winning me five. To celebrate, I bought Lily an ice-cream cone.

After a few more races, I realized that I could never make much more than I won if I didn't place more than two dollars down at a time. I was also spending quite a lot on Lily—hot dogs, candy, more ice cream—to keep her entertained. I decided that if I was willing to take the risk of traveling across the country with a child that wasn't mine, I could put down all the money I had left on one bet. I chose carefully, finally deciding on a horse called Red Rockets. Red was an auspicious color for the Chinese, and the rockets reminded me of fireworks, which were also Chinese.

I sat Lily down on a bench. "Wait here until I get back," I told her.

She nodded, the corners of her mouth stained with chocolate.

When I got to the front of the line at the betting window, I hesitated only a moment before placing all I had left, twenty dollars, on Red Rockets to win. The fact that it was a large, strapping horse the color of dark blood made me even more confident. I ran to the rail with everyone else to watch the race unfold.

Red Rockets burst out of the gate ahead of the other horses. My heart was in my throat as I shouted with the others in the crowd. Then it began to descend to my stomach as the horse I had placed all my hopes on fell back and drifted behind the pack. It ended dead last, in a limp. Something seemed to be wrong with its front hoof.

The man next to me shook his head. "That one's going to the glue factory," he said.

"Sorry?" I turned to him.

"I've been coming to this track for fifteen years and it always ends the same way."

"But it looks well," I said. The horse was tossing its head as if wanting to break free.

"Can't feel any pain with the drugs. Too bad, that was a nice horse." The man turned to the next page of his racing form.

I couldn't believe that this was the end for an animal that moments before had been alive and defiant. But as I watched the horse being loaded into the equine ambulance and driven off the track, I understood that its end was also my end. I had no money left. Lily and I were now as good as homeless.

Lily. I rushed back to where I had left her on the bench near the betting windows. She wasn't there. All I saw was the crumpled wrapper from a bar of candy I had bought her earlier. I searched among the other benches and inside where people could watch the races on television screens.

"Have you seen a little girl? About three years old? In a red coat?" I asked, but got only shakes of the head.

Looking around, I began to notice how seedy the crowd here was. Men, mostly old men, who looked like they hadn't shaved or held a decent job in years. Had one of them taken Lily? What would they do to her?

For a moment I thought about calling the police. I wanted to put that off as long as possible. But I was beginning to think that this was where everything would end. And it didn't matter, as long as Lily was safe.

I had always thought that Lily occupied a special place in my consciousness. I could spot her in a playground full of children. I would be in another room in the Templeton-Walkers' apartment and know that she had woken up, although I couldn't hear her. I had felt this connection even before I had taken care of her, from the moment I had spotted her in the park.

Now I saw her down by the racetrack, a patch of red in the midst of the gray crowd, my good luck charm.

"Lily!" I shouted.

She turned toward me, her face pale above her red coat.

When I reached her, I captured her in a forceful hug. I wanted to convince myself that she was there and alive but she struggled to be turned loose.

"She was all alone," a man nearby said, in Mandarin.

He was Chinese and middle-aged; something about his face reminded me of my uncle. It sagged in the same places, drooped around the eyes and mouth. But there was kindness in those eyes, too, as he regarded us.

"I only left her for a minute," I said, defensive.

"What are you doing here?"

"What, can't women gamble?" I felt bolder speaking in Mandarin and acted toward him the way I might to Old Chou or one of my old coworkers.

"I meant, the racetrack is no place for a child."

I couldn't argue with that. Instead, I put Lily down but kept my hands on her shoulders to keep her from moving away. "It was our first time here."

"Did you learn anything?"

"That gambling doesn't pay?"

He nodded in approval. "Then you've learned a valuable lesson that takes other people years to learn."

"Haven't you learned it?"

"I learned it once. Certain circumstances have made me come back. You see people like us everywhere."

I supposed he meant the few other Chinese I had seen that day at the racetrack. I wondered where they had come from, whether they all lived in this town or congregated at the track on the weekends.

"Are you from here?" I asked.

He nodded. "My wife and I own a restaurant."

"Looking for a waitress?" I asked, half joking. An image filled my mind: me sweeping the floor at the end of the day while Lily played off to the side of a dining room. Then I pictured myself and Lily living in a small house in the middle of a field, like those I had seen from the bus window. I quickly blacked it out. "How is business here?"

"It's good. We started twenty years ago with almost nothing and now our place is the best Chinese restaurant around. Of course, there aren't many others besides the take-out places." He paused. "Where did you come from?"

Ni cong nali laide? It could mean either where had I just come from or where I was from—where I was born. I chose to interpret it as the former.

"New York," I said. "We were taking a bus, but . . ."

"But?"

"We ran out of money," I said. There was no use in telling him the entire story.

"Is she all right?" the man asked. He was looking at Lily, who was dangling from my arms as if she didn't have the strength to stand upright anymore.

"She's fine," I said. "She's just—"

Lily's head jerked forward and she threw up all over the ground. Both the man and I stared at the puddle of vomit, which was streaked brown from chocolate, the last thing she'd eaten. Then Lily began to cry.

"It's okay," I hushed, cradling her head.

The man offered us a napkin, which I used to wipe Lily's face. I noticed that her face was burning up, but tears hardly came from her eyes. Her entire body was so hot that she should have been drenched in sweat, yet her skin was dry. When she looked at me, her gaze was glassy and as uncomprehending as that of a porcelain doll.

I clutched her to my chest and rocked back and forth to quiet her down. Outwardly I must have looked in control, like any mother trying to ease the pain of a child, but inside I was panicking. There was something terribly wrong with Lily. I tried to remember any other time she had been sick. Jane had mentioned colds, but I had never been around to witness what she had done about them. What was happening to Lily now seemed far worse.

"What's the matter with her?" the man asked. I had almost forgotten he was there.

"She's very sick. I don't know what to do," I admitted. "She needs help."

"Should we take her to the hospital?"

"No hospital!" I didn't care what I sounded like; he probably thought we were illegals anyway.

"We'll take her to my house then," the man said quickly. "My wife will know what to do."

I looked up at him over Lily's head.

"My name is Feng," he said, offering his hand.

I hesitated for a second before taking it. He helped us to our feet and I let him carry Lily out of the racetrack grounds and into the parking lot to his car. I got in the backseat with her.

At first I was afraid that Feng was taking us to the hospital, but we passed the main part of town without stopping. It seemed like we were heading toward the suburbs. We passed rows of houses prefaced by neat lawns, dizzying in their alikeness.

Outside, the afternoon light was rapidly fading. I placed one hand on Lily's chest, measuring each fluttering breath. I kept my eyes fixed on the back of Feng's head, the close-cropped graying hair, the rough sunburned neck. This was what it must feel like to trust a stranger, I thought; you start with something small. I remembered when Jane had first trusted me to watch Lily in the park alone. By now the only thing she could trust me to do was to try to keep Lily safe. But, within a few days, I didn't know if that was possible anymore.

Chapter Sixteen

We stopped in front of a modest-sized house that reminded me of my aunt and uncle's place in New Jersey. But though it was made of newer materials, it looked less permanent, less cared for, as if whoever built it hadn't planned on sticking around for very long. There were rosebushes like my aunt's in the front yard but no one had bothered to prepare them for winter so they looked patchy and thin. A light shone from the upper left window, and I saw Feng glance up at it after the engine died. I carried Lily inside after him.

He clicked on the hall light. Through an archway I saw a living room where the furniture was plain and the carpet the color of thin porridge. There was none of the confused clutter of my aunt and uncle's home, with their mix of Eastern and Western objects and the photos of all the places they'd been.

"Wait here," Feng said. "I need to talk to my wife first and prepare her. She's not well these days. But she'll know what to do."

I nodded and balanced Lily against my hip. She was awake now, although her face remained hot. I pushed her hair back from her face. Any other time she would be irritated by my fussiness, but now her lack of reaction worried me. *Please, Lily,* I begged. *Please be okay.*

Creaks from above indicated that someone was coming down the stairs. Feng began to speak to someone in English. I could hear snatches of his side of the conversation, though not how she responded: ". . . young woman . . . sick child . . . no hospital . . . nowhere else to go. . . ."

Feng came into the hall, followed by an American woman whose sallow, pinch-lipped face did not appear very welcoming. Her hair looked pale from age rather than color, and a bathrobe patterned with faded roses was wrapped around her thin frame. I would have thought she had just risen from bed if she didn't look uncommonly tense, as if she were waiting for a doorbell to ring, or something worse, perhaps a stone to come crashing through the front window.

"This is my wife, Christine," Feng said.

Before I could respond, Christine stepped forward and placed her hand on Lily's forehead.

"She threw up earlier," Feng informed her.

"What has she eaten today?" Christine asked.

I told her about the vending machine chips and cookies from the bus station, the popcorn, ice cream, hot dogs, and candy from the racetrack.

"No wonder she's sick," Christine observed. She said to Feng, "We might as well put her in Paul's room."

Feng and I brought Lily upstairs to a room at the end of the hall. In a moment Christine joined us with a wet washcloth, a bottle of pills, a glass of water, and a thermometer.

"Temperature first," she said.

"Open," I told Lily in English. She acted like she didn't understand me.

Before I could do anything, Christine reached out and grasped Lily's chin. "Open your mouth," she ordered.

Lily obeyed, but when the thermometer was put under her tongue, she began to cry and struggle in my arms.

"Hold her," Christine said.

Like Lily, I followed orders. "I'm sorry," I murmured to Lily as I held her arms and legs down. She stared resentfully back, her mouth in the exact shape of an upside-down smile as it clamped around the thermometer. I was heartened by the fact that she was bothering to look cross at me again.

Christine shook something out of the bottle into the palm of her hand. "It's baby aspirin," she said. "It's perfectly safe. I take it every day for my heart."

I made Lily swallow the aspirin. She dribbled most of the glass of water down her front.

"Now she needs to rest," Christine said.

Together, she and I undressed Lily and tucked her in. Worn out from crying, Lily lay quietly with her eyes closed. I couldn't tell if her face was flushed from fever or exhaustion. Christine bathed Lily's forehead and limbs with the washcloth.

"She'll be all right." Christine turned to me. "Have you eaten yet?"

Hearing those words made my eyes and the back of my throat burn. It was the first thing my grandmother would say upon my coming home in the evening: *Chile ma?* Fatigue turned time on its head and for a moment I thought my grandmother was still alive.

I shook my head, grasping at the last threads of politeness I had left. "No, thank you. It has been a long day. We will go to sleep now."

Lily fell into an exhausted sleep but I couldn't do the same. I lay next to her on the narrow bed, counting her each breath as though it were a valuable coin. Now that we were safe, in a house instead of on the road, I could start to think that things would get better. Then the oddness of the situation penetrated my sense of relief. I had trusted Feng and Christine to help me, and perhaps even more peculiar, they had invited me into their home without any question.

Hours passed. It was the time of night when everything felt unreal and dead. I thought of the rows of similar-looking houses we had passed on our way here and wondered if I were the only person awake for miles. Maybe I was the one who had died. I wouldn't be surprised if heaven in America consisted of streets where everyone's houses looked the same.

I turned on a small lamp on the bedside table, holding my breath at the click, but Lily didn't stir. What I saw of my surroundings made me think of my cousin's room at my aunt and uncle's house. The twin bed, the desk with its plastic cup of writing utensils, the single, straight-backed chair all indicated that this was a child's room, although it looked like no one had slept here for a while. There were no books on the shelves that said anything about its former occupant, or photos on the walls. The lack of photos here and in the living room below puzzled me. This was the first Western house I had been in that didn't have any pictures of a wedding or a graduation or a beloved child, as proof of a life well lived.

Christine had called it Paul's room. I guessed that Feng and Christine's son had grown up and left home years ago. There was something about them that had reminded me of my aunt and uncle, the look of a middle-aged couple abandoned by their children.

I hadn't heard any movement outside the room since Lily and I had been left to sleep. Feng and Christine must have gone to bed, not concerned that the interloper in their house might steal something. Then a soft knock at the door nearly made me jump. The door opened to reveal Christine in the hall, looking like a ghost. Then she moved into the room and the spectral effect vanished. In the circle of lamplight, she was merely an aging woman in her house slippers.

"How is the little girl?" Christine asked.

"She is sleeping."

"And you?"

"No."

A faint smile crossed her face. "Neither can I. I'm going to make a cup of tea if you want to join me."

I followed Christine downstairs to the kitchen, where she fixed two mugs. She had added so much milk and sugar to mine that it made me think of sweet bathwater, but still I sipped it. We sat across from each other at the table in silence. Christine seemed uncomfortable in her own house, not looking at anything in the room, tapping her fingers against the tabletop.

"You shouldn't worry," Christine said. "Paul had plenty of fevers when he was a child."

"Paul is your son?" I asked.

Christine nodded.

"Where is he now?"

"He's dead."

I knew I was supposed to say *I'm sorry*. I had said it before, to Jane when she had told me about her baby that had never been born. But in this circumstance, sorry sounded empty of meaning. "I am very sorry," I said, only making it worse.

"Why? You didn't know him."

For a moment her directness confused me.

"Please excuse me," Christine said after a while. "I say the first thing that comes into my head these days. There's no time for anything else. So many people have said they're sorry. The neighbors, Paul's old teachers, people at the grocery store, when they never spoke to us before. It is strange to me that you would say you're sorry about the death of someone you didn't know."

"I would like to know," I said.

Both excitement and fear came into Christine's eyes, as if she were afraid that I would change my mind. "Do you want to know what he looked like?"

"Yes."

"Wait a minute."

She came back into the room with a wallet-sized photo that she laid down before me on the table. Paul didn't look like his mother or father, American or Chinese. He just looked handsome as only a young man in a military uniform can, no matter what cause he is fighting for. His shoulders were straight and square, and his face looked very young.

"How old was he?" I asked.

"Twenty-one. His father and I didn't want him to join the army, but that was the only way he could go to college. I told him we'd think of some way to pay, but he didn't want our help."

I hadn't thought that Feng and Christine might not be able to send their son to college. They owned their own business, a house, a car—back in China they would be considered rich. But I had no one to compare them to in America other than my aunt and uncle, or Jane and Richard. I didn't know what families were like here.

"But he helped his country," I said.

Christine's laugh broke in her throat. "If you want to believe that. Feng's mother used to tell him that if he weren't careful, he would lose Paul to American ideas and traditions. She never considered that those were my traditions. I wish I could tell her now that Feng and I have truly lost our son to this country." She paused. "He was in Iraq."

I remembered, back in New York, seeing headlines that marched across the front page of the newspaper, proclaiming the death of one or two American soldiers each day. Christine's son must have been one of them. I must have passed a newsstand or stepped over a newspaper in the hallway of the Templeton-Walkers' apartment building on the day it was announced that he had died.

"His helicopter crashed in the desert and five soldiers died. It wasn't shot down. It was an accident."

"An accident?"

"You sound disappointed."

"No, I—"

"That's all right. Most people are disappointed when I tell them. They want to hear that there was a big explosion caused by a grenade or guns. They don't want to hear that it was like being in a plane crash or a car crash. That it could have happened here."

"But it didn't," I said. I imagined a fireball in a blue sky and charred pieces of debris falling to the ground below. But the land I pictured was not a desert, which I had never seen before with my own eyes. Instead, I pictured the endless fields I had traveled through for the past two days. If you squinted, they looked like rolling hills of golden sand.

Then I thought of the Vietnam vet I had seen in the Chicago bus station. Would Paul have ended up like him if he had been injured but lived? Or would dying be better than living as a crazed, bitter old man?

"We used to have lots of photos of Paul all around the house," Christine said. "In the front hall we had a picture of him when he was eight. He was playing an Indian for Thanksgiving and wore a headdress made out of a feather and one of Feng's neckties. Next to that was a picture of him in his Little League baseball uniform; there were grass stains on it that I could never get out. And then there was a picture of him when he got his driver's license, standing next to our car which he never liked to drive because it was too old. I remember them all."

"What happened to them?"

"I gave them away. Less than a week after the funeral, I packed all of Paul's things up and gave them to the Salvation Army. Feng didn't like my behavior. He thought I was being irrational. But that's the only way I can be. You can't tell someone else how to feel."

For the first time, I wondered what my grandmother had gone through when she had learned of my parents' death. Had she wept for weeks after, screaming at the heavens for taking away her only child? Or had she been like Christine, oddly calm, almost detached, as she discussed her dead son? No, my grandmother wouldn't have cried. She would have pulled herself together, because she had me to look after. I was too young to have helped her bear her pain, but she had helped me with mine, even if I hadn't known it at the time.

"You have your husband to help you," I said.

"Feng's sad about what happened, but we feel it in different ways. We're always going to be alone in our grief. They say the loss of a child either brings a couple closer together or drives them apart. I don't know which it will be for us. People here tell us to go to church, but we aren't religious like our neighbors. I stay and sit in Paul's room, and Feng goes to the racetrack. I guess it's a good thing he did today."

"Yes," I said. "He saved us."

"Your daughter will be all right," Christine said softly. "Her fever will be gone in the morning."

"No."

"Really, you have to trust me on this—"

"No," I heard myself saying. I could not lie about my relationship with Lily to a mother who had lost her son. "She's not my daughter."

"I didn't think she was," Christine replied, to my surprise. "You don't look anything alike."

I had never heard anyone say this to me before. Whenever I had taken Lily to the park, when we were walking down the street, people would look from her black head to mine and assume she was my daughter. I had also believed there was a special bond between Lily and me that even strangers could see. Now I thought maybe I had been imagining things. And that everyone else was deluded, grasping at any hint that there was a meaningful connection between two people.

"You're right," I said slowly. "We're not related. But I take care of her."

"Ah." Christine sounded pleased. "I knew you had a close relationship, but I didn't think you were her mother. Other than the fact that she doesn't look like you, of course. But you don't look like a mother. You don't know what to do with her when she's sick. You haven't sat at her bedside when she's had an ear infection or a bad dream."

"I didn't want to take her to the hospital," I said.

"I don't think she was as sick as you thought she was. If the situation was that serious, you would have done the right thing."

Christine had more confidence in me than I had. Would I have taken Lily to the hospital and given up any chance for us to stay together? No matter the true state of Lily's health, I had believed she could be dying. I could have killed her. At any point along our trip, I could have abandoned her at a bus stop or left her with strangers. I had been capable of that, and that awful power left me feeling numb.

"If she's not your daughter," Christine said, "then whose daughter is she?"

"No one's."

"What do you mean? Everyone has parents. You mean you don't know?"

A confession rose in my throat and caught at the tip of my tongue. It wanted to fall, like the relief of rain after a long drought. Now I understood why Christine had told me about Paul's death. I hadn't needed to pry among her belongings for clues or listen carefully to every nuance in her voice. There wasn't time for that.

And so I told her. I told Christine how I had first met Jane and Lily in the park, how I had started babysitting, and been let go from my job days after discovering that my grandmother had died. That was the only time any expression crossed Christine's face, when I had told her about receiving Old Luo's letter. Otherwise, she appeared impassive, only occasionally nodding as if to show that she was listening. She seemed to show no judgment.

"Where are you taking her now?" she asked after I finished my story.

"California." Earlier, when I'd said it to the girl on the bus, it had felt like our destiny. But now, some time later, in the early hours of another day, it hardly seemed possible. "We were supposed to go to California."

"You can still go."

I shook my head, gripping my mug of tea, which had grown cold.

After a moment Christine rose to her feet. "We should go to bed now. Everything will be fine in the morning. You'll know what to do." She looked down at the photo of Paul on the table, and then pushed it toward me in one sharp movement. "You can have this if you want."

I was startled by this gesture. Why would I want to have the picture of someone I didn't know, as if he were a friend or a sweetheart? Looking again at the photo, I was reminded of my parents, of their wedding picture. There was nothing about my parents' faces that had hinted at any early tragedy, or hardship, or even happiness. In his picture, Paul's eyes had the same blankness. He had no idea what was going to happen to him.

"Yes," I said. "I would like to have it."

Upstairs, I placed the photo on the table next to the bed, facedown so the young man's eyes wouldn't haunt me. Lily was sleeping peacefully, her eyelashes soft against her cool cheeks. I lay on top of the blanket, shielding her with my body without touching her. I wanted to protect her from any bad dreams the rest of the night might bring.

Chapter Seventeen

I'm walking down one of the winding streets in Fuzhou from my childhood. Yet now I am a grown-up; every step I take covers more ground than it did when I was little, and the stone walls no longer look so impenetrably high. The sky is a sunless gray, and the wind weaves through the hanging roots of the banyan trees.

Although my feet seem to know where to take me, my mind is blank. But as I turn the corner, my stride lengthens even more, and so does my memory. Through an open gate, I see a two-story Western-style house with green shutters. The panes of glass in the windows are intact and no tiles are missing from the eaves. I recognize this house as mine. I am returning home after a long absence.

I pass through the gate into a poet's garden. Willows surround a small pond filled with carp whose scales ripple like silken scarves beneath the water. The plum trees are in bloom, shedding snowy petals over the clipped grass. Someone has been taking care of this place—although, as I look at my hands, I see that it hasn't been me. My hands are slender and pale, like those of a lady who stays out of the sun.

At the touch of my hand, the front door of the house swings open. I enter a room that is intended for receiving guests. A fireplace graces one end, made of smooth white marble like a woman's limbs. Rosewood furniture, burnished a deep red-gold, glows like a sunset. The shutters of the windows are open, and the plum trees in the garden are visible through the panes of glass that are as thin as sheets of rice paper. I walk across the polished floor and sit down, gingerly, on a rosewood chair. It is less comfortable than I expect, hard and unconforming to human flesh.

Now I become aware of the deep silence in the house, only punctuated by a clock ticking on the mantelpiece. Again I have the sense that I am returning home after a long time away. I feel a tinge of disappointment that no one is here to greet me. I look around the room and feel that a child has walked across this floor. I instinctively know that I have a husband and a child somewhere.

As if summoned by that thought, a young man walks into the room. He is tall and wears a military uniform. He is Paul, Feng and Christine's son. He doesn't look quite so young, and the sternness in his face is plainly etched in lines around his eyes and mouth. But somehow I know he is my husband.

Your child is dead, Paul informs me.

I don't believe you, I say.

He turns his back, and when he faces me again, I can see that he is carrying something in his arms. The limp body of a little girl whose dark hair spills over his hands.

She's sleeping, I say.

No, she will never wake. She died because you left.

I stand in front of him, the child's body between us. *Give
her to me,* I say.

No.

She's mine.

I grab hold of her body, but he won't let go. We pull back
and forth, and then abruptly the child is as light as air. I look
down and see a plastic doll lying at our feet, the head separated from the body. I bend to the ground, gathering the doll
parts into my arms, weeping.

~   ~   ~

For a moment, in the darkness, I didn't know where I was. I
could be in my boardinghouse room in Chinatown, or on the
bus in the middle of nowhere. Then I remembered that I was
in someone else's bedroom. Tears were still wet on my cheeks.

I rolled over and reached for Lily. She was lying beside me,
so still that I was afraid to touch her. I feared that if I did, I
would find that the worst had come true. Finally I brought
myself to place my hand on her forehead. It was cool, and when
I pulled back the blanket, I found that her fever had broken.
Christine had been right. Maybe she was right about other
things, too. That I would know what to do.

Grainy predawn light was coming through the window, and
my face was dry now. I rose and pushed back the curtain to
see the first signs of the day's life. Birds flew from the eaves
down to the lawn. A boy rode by on a bicycle and a newspaper seemed to hit the front doorstep before his arm could
finish its sweep through the sky. Gradually, lights were coming on in the houses across the street. I didn't have much time.

I took a pencil from the desk but there was nothing to write
on except the back of the photo Christine had given me. I

turned the photo right side up and stared at the face of the young man whom I had never met in real life. No, I didn't need a photo; I already had his face memorized. Quickly I flipped it over and wrote down Jane's name and phone number and left it on the desk. There was nothing I would take from this place.

I stood up and looked at Lily, willing her to open her eyes. I couldn't wake her; she would have to do it without my prompting. But she slept on, oblivious to my presence.

I slipped outside into the hall and closed the door softly behind me. I didn't hear anything from Feng and Christine's room. For a moment I hesitated, wondering if I should wake them or leave a more substantial note. But there was nothing more I could say. And perhaps it would be better, if they were questioned by the police, to be able to say, truthfully, that I had snuck out in the early morning.

I let myself out of the house as dawn was brightening into day. I remembered the direction we had come from last night in the car and headed that way. The rising sun was behind me. I could feel its warmth hitting the points of my elbows and the backs of my knees. I could hear the hum of distant traffic getting louder in my ears.

Acknowledgments

I would like to thank the following people for their help on this book: my agent, Shana Kelly; my editor, Jamison Stoltz; my teachers at New York University, especially Chuck Wachtel and Paule Marshall; my readers Kay Kim, Samuel Park, Angie Mei, Zoraya Nambi, and Neil Gladstone; and, most of all, my family.

A BLACK CAT READING GROUP GUIDE
BY BARBARA PUTNAM

HAPPY FAMILY

WENDY LEE

ABOUT THIS GUIDE

We hope that these discussion questions
will enhance your reading group's exploration
of Wendy Lee's *Happy Family*. They are
meant to stimulate discussion, offer new viewpoints,
and enrich your enjoyment of the book.

More reading group guides and additional information,
including summaries, author tours, and author sites for
other fine Black Cat titles, may be found on
our Web site, www.groveatlantic.com.

QUESTIONS FOR DISCUSSION

1. In the Preface, Hua writes to Lily: "I hope that by now your parents have forgiven me for loving you as much as they did. If they are still married, maybe they would even thank me" (p. 5). Is this a letter you think Hua actually sent? If so, how likely is it that Lily's parents would have forgiven Hua? Or thanked her?

2. When Hua learns that her grandparents had once owned a large Western-style house, she wonders why she had never been told. Her grandmother shrugs and says, "What use would that be? What's lost is lost" (p. 29). Is it understandable that Hua can feel homesick for this house she has never even entered? How is "What's lost is lost" applicable to other moments in the novel? At one point Hua herself tells Jane that it was fate that led to Lily's adoption. Do you see this resignation to fate as a particularly Asian attitude?

3. "The Chengs are known for bending in the breeze, for giving in to others. That's how they get what they want. And that's what you have to do when you get to America. You have to be what other people want you to be, before you can be yourself" (p. 33). Does her grandmother's advice to Hua seem well-founded for an immigrant? At what cost? Do you think Hua is guided by it? When?

4. Is Jane foolishly trusting, even from early on, leaving Lily with Hua at the playground while she runs an errand? (p. 58) When does Hua herself take leaps of faith? How is she rewarded? Are there times you think she is naïve, insouciant, or careless? Have you made decisions, leaps of faith, that went against caution and conventional wisdom?

5. Talk about some of the complicated issues involved in foreign adoptions. Why is it that Jane went to the trouble and expense of adopting a Chinese baby instead of an American? Hua says about Lily, "There must be some kind of shame attached to her that no one would ever know, least of all her new parents. She had no background, no history, except for what was in her new home" (p. 55). What are the cultural and legal questions she refers to? Hua says later, "She'll grow up knowing nothing about her homeland. She'll be worse than those American-born Chinese" (p. 107). Do you agree?

6. In the Chinatowns of New York and other cities, transplants can nourish their memories and reinforce their Chinese identity. Else-

where, immigrants may be forced to assimilate. Which atmosphere do you think serves them better in the end?

7. What is the basis for this comment of Hua's about Lily, "She, for one, would be carrying a lot of weight on her shoulders when she grew up"? (p. 164) How is it related to Hua's question, "Were all children, in some way, a form of redemption for their parents?" (p.164). Do you agree with this statement? Why or why not?

8. In Lee's novel, how does the geography of New York City become part of the story? What does Hua seek in her perambulations? What reminds her of her childhood in China?

9. How does Hua's playacting lead to a kind of identity theft? (Think of her in Jane's bedroom and at the playground. In fact, think of her subterfuge at the airport.) Is this a process that happens in stages? In forging a new identity, how is she writing her own story?

10. Talk about the title, *Happy Family*. Do you gather that Richard and Jane have ever been truly "happy"? What are the other marriages like in the book? Her uncle and aunt? Her own parents? Does the California setting offer new hope? How?

11. What do you learn about what it is to be Chinese American? Do you see inevitable differences between Asian immigrants and, say, European ones? What do you think happens to Hua after the end of the book? Do you think she will succeed in her new life?

SUGGESTIONS FOR FURTHER READING:

Hunger by Lan Samantha Chang; *Bone* by Fae M. Ng; *Typical American* by Gish Jen; *China Boy* by Gus Lee; *American Visa* by Wang Ping; *The Woman Warrior* by Maxine Hong Kingston